RED TED
AND THE
LOST
THINGS

For Emile, Elsie, and Emma
M. R.

For the lost and found of Dalston
J. S.

Text copyright © 2009 by Michael Rosen
Illustrations copyright © 2009 by Joel Stewart

First U.S. paperback edition 2009

Library of Congress Cataloging-in-Publication Data

Rosen, Michael.
Red Ted and the lost things / Michael Rosen ; illustrated by Joel Stewart. —1st ed.
p. cm.
Summary: When a teddy bear is accidentally left on the seat of a train, he uses his ingenuity —and some new friends —to search for the little girl who lost him.
ISBN 978-0-7636-4537-3 (hardcover)
[1. Teddy bears —Fiction. 2. Toys —Fiction. 3. Lost and found possessions —Fiction.]
I. Stewart, Joel, ill. II. Title.
PZ7.R71867Re 2010
[E —dc22   2009002992

ISBN 978-0-7636-4624-0 (paperback)

10 11 12 13 14 SCP 10 9 8 7 6 4 3 2

Printed in Humen, Dongguan, China

This book was typeset in OPTI Typo and Regular Joe.
The illustrations were done in mixed media.

Candlewick Press
99 Dover Street
Somerville, Massachusetts 02144

visit us at www.candlewick.com

RED TED
AND THE
LOST
THINGS

MICHAEL ROSEN

ILLUSTRATED BY
JOEL STEWART

CANDLEWICK PRESS

One day a little bear named Red Ted was left on a train. He found himself being put on a shelf by a Man in a Hat.

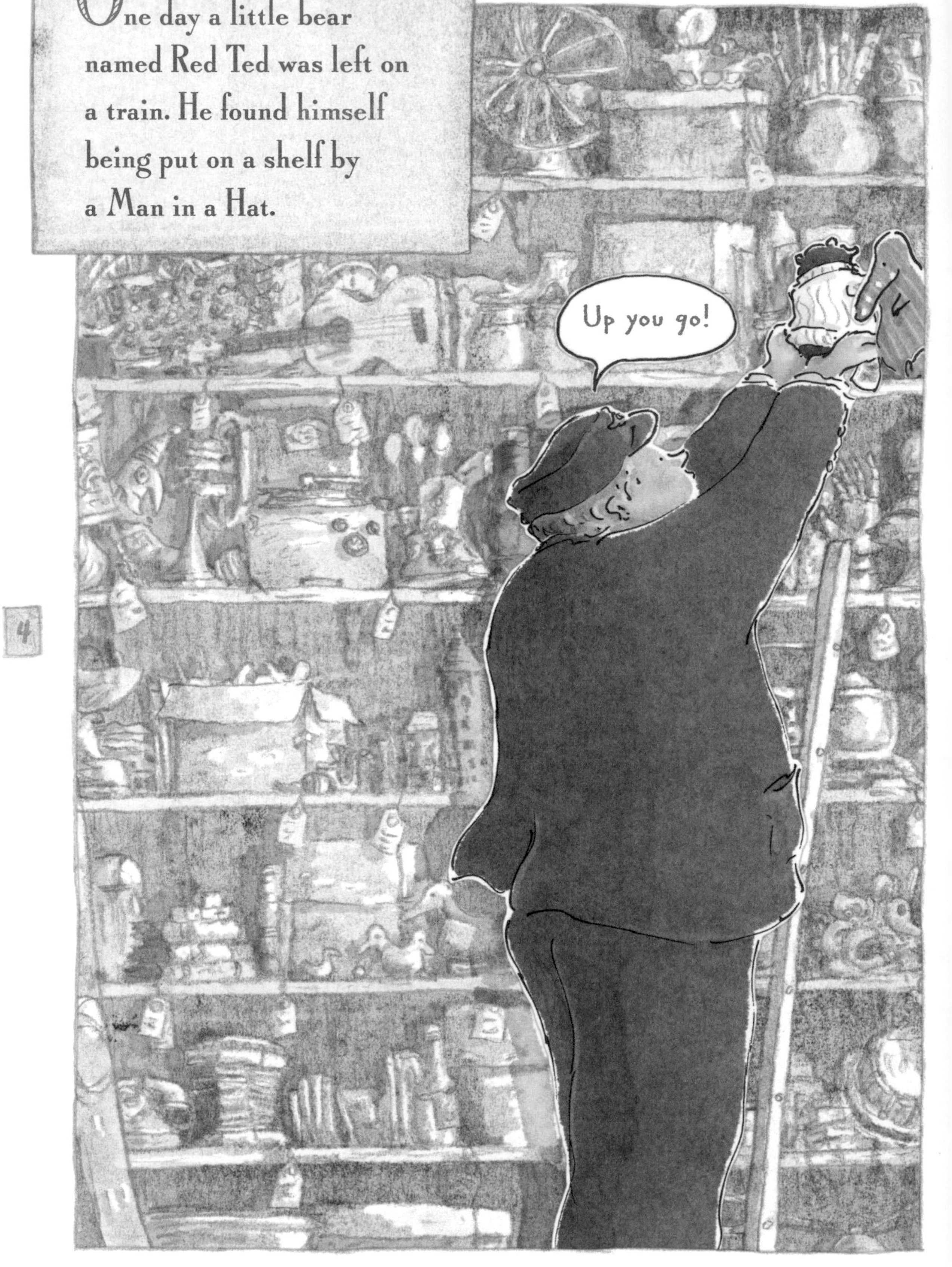
Up you go!

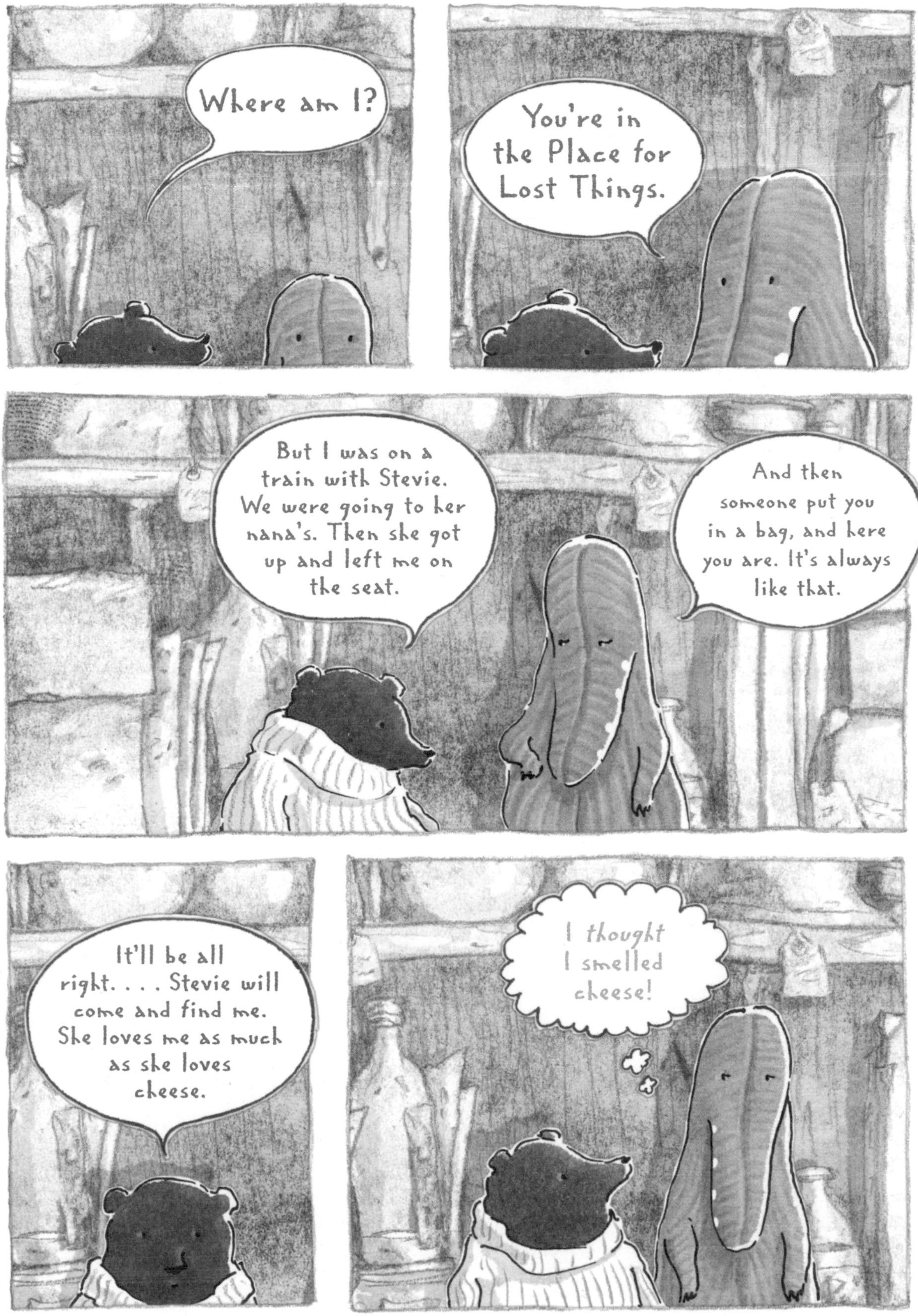
Where am I?
You're in the Place for Lost Things.
But I was on a train with Stevie. We were going to her nana's. Then she got up and left me on the seat.
And then someone put you in a bag, and here you are. It's always like that.
It'll be all right. . . . Stevie will come and find me. She loves me as much as she loves cheese.
I *thought* I smelled cheese!

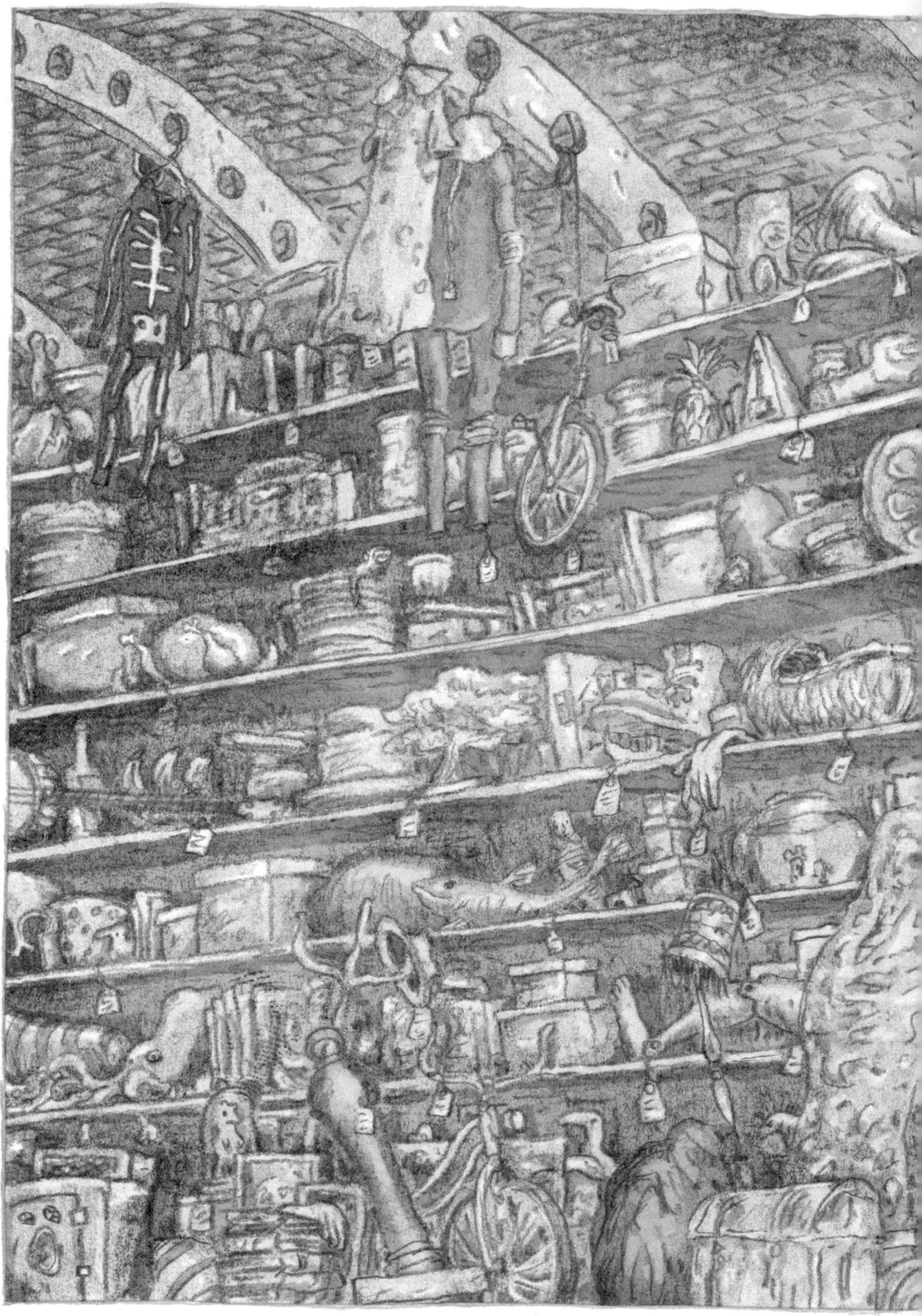

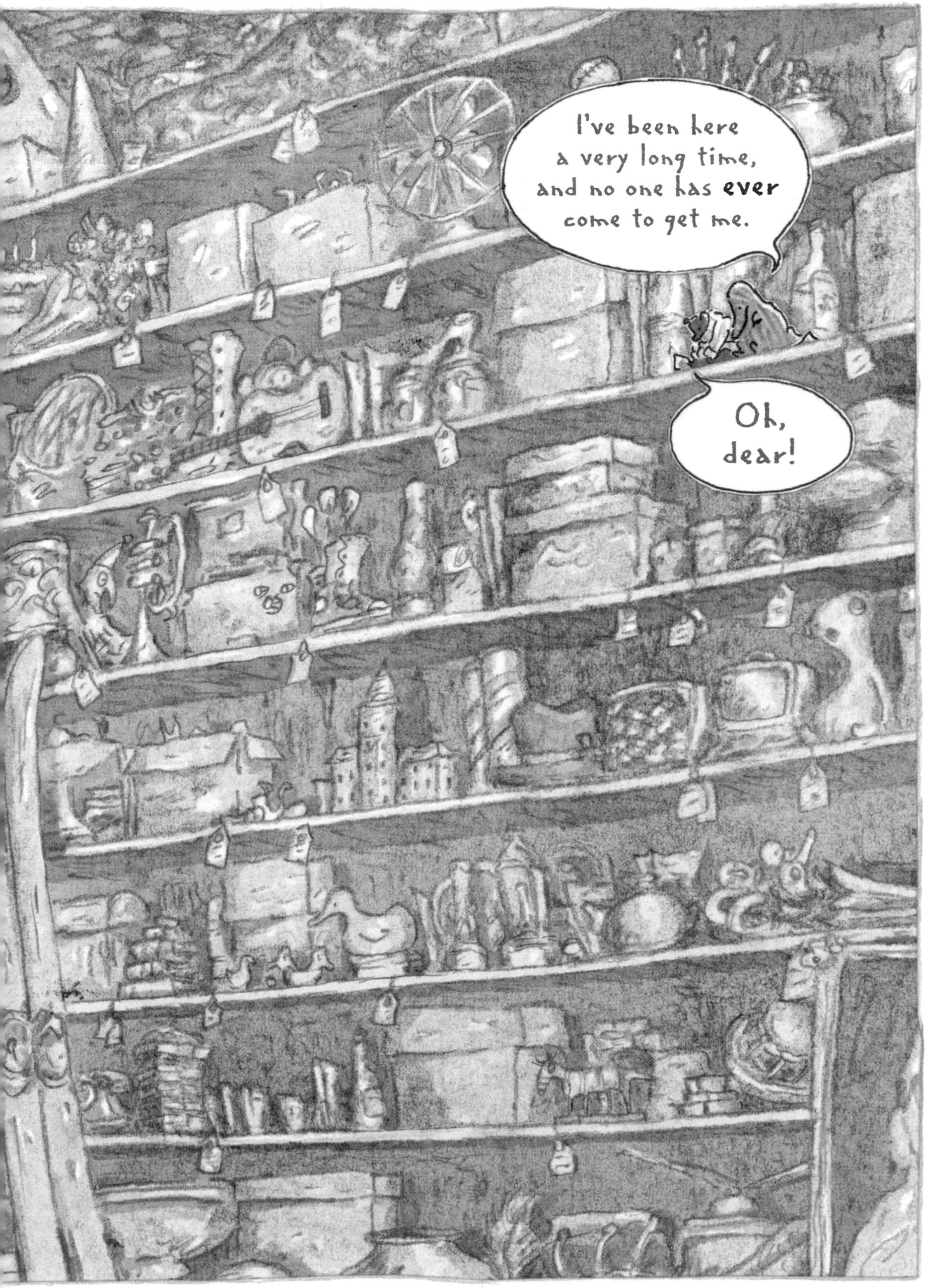
I've been here
a very long time,
and no one has **ever**
come to get me.
Oh,
dear!

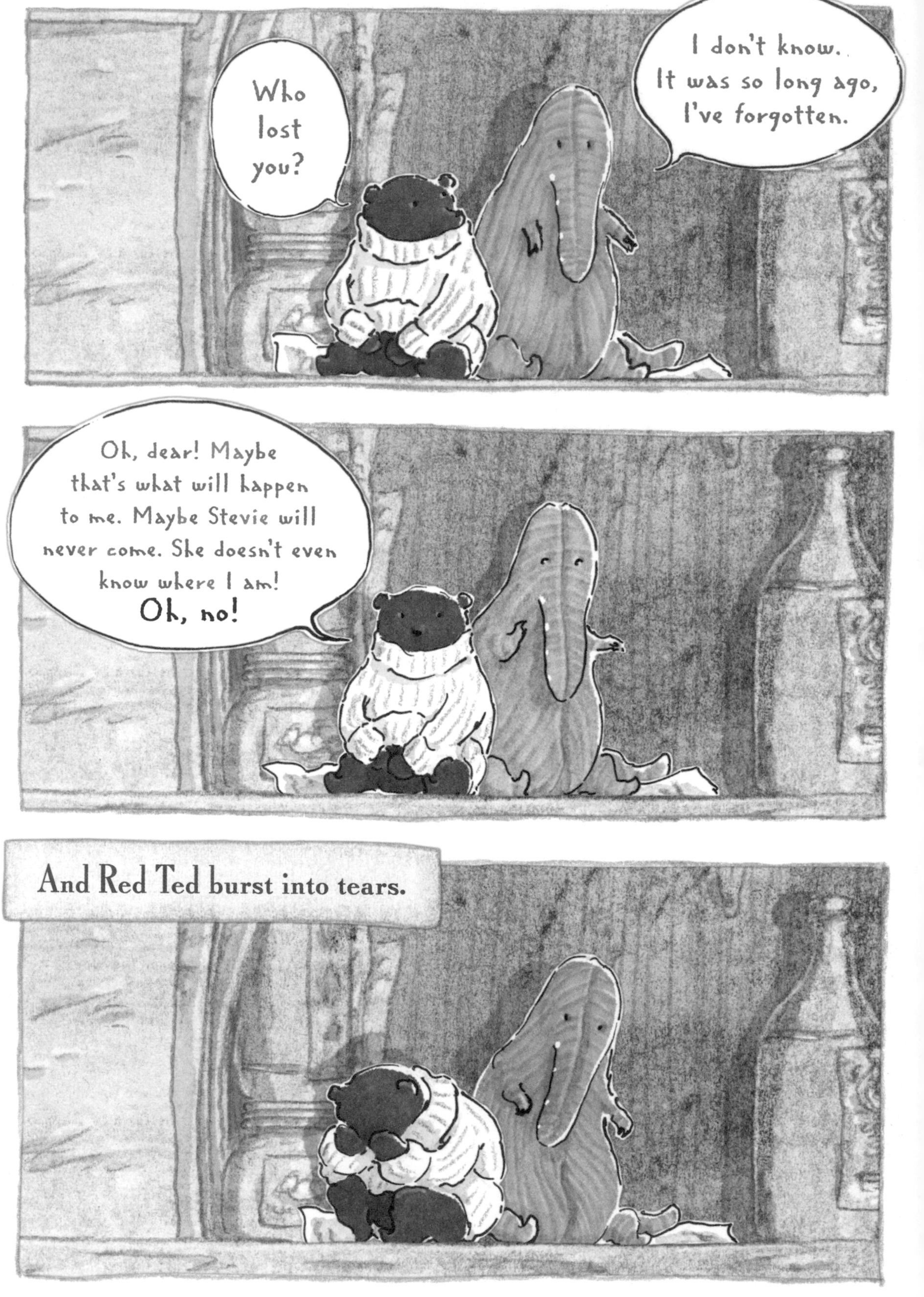
Who lost you?
I don't know. It was so long ago, I've forgotten.
Oh, dear! Maybe that's what will happen to me. Maybe Stevie will never come. She doesn't even know where I am!
Oh, no!
And Red Ted burst into tears.

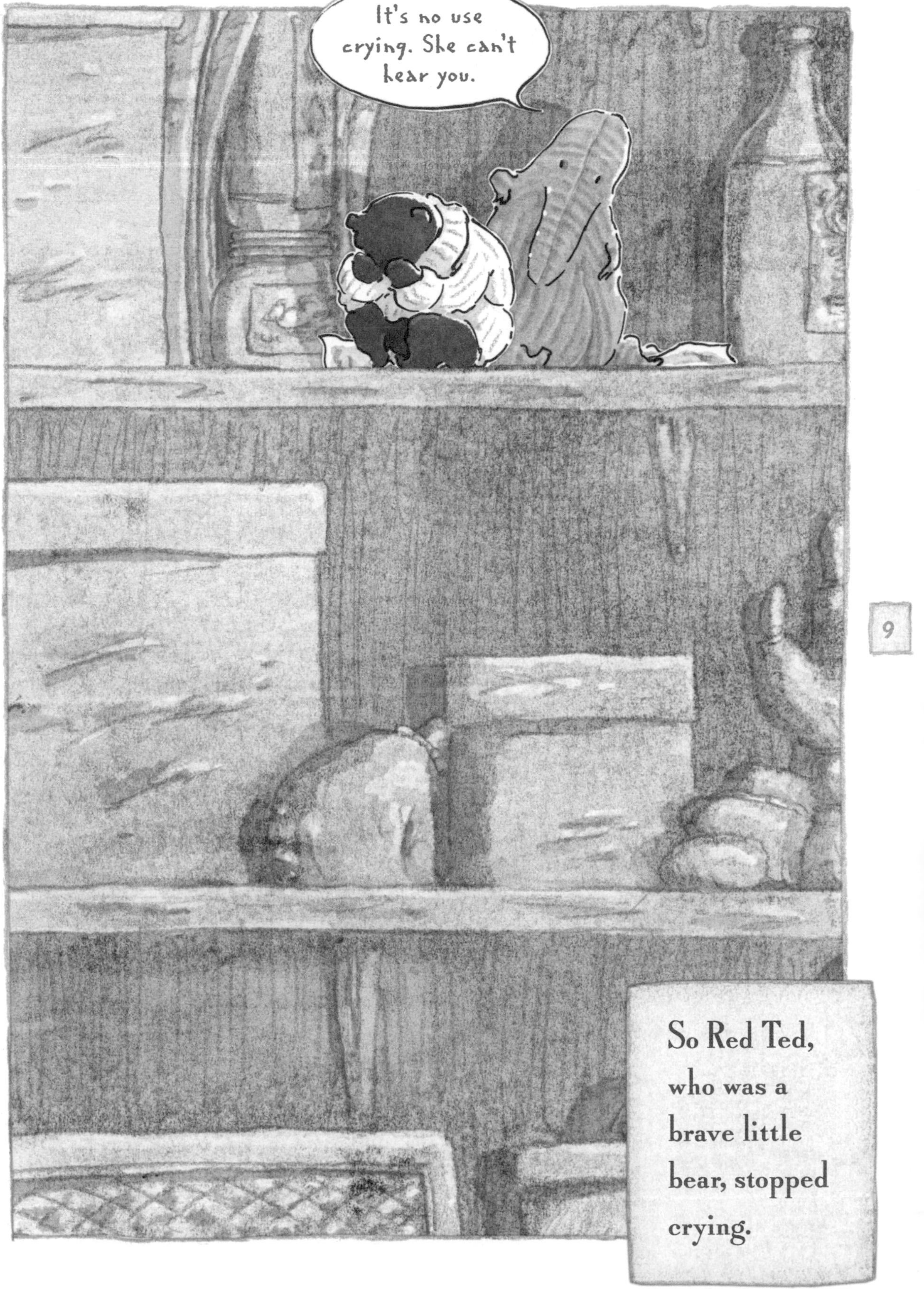
It's no use crying. She can't hear you.

So Red Ted, who was a brave little bear, stopped crying.

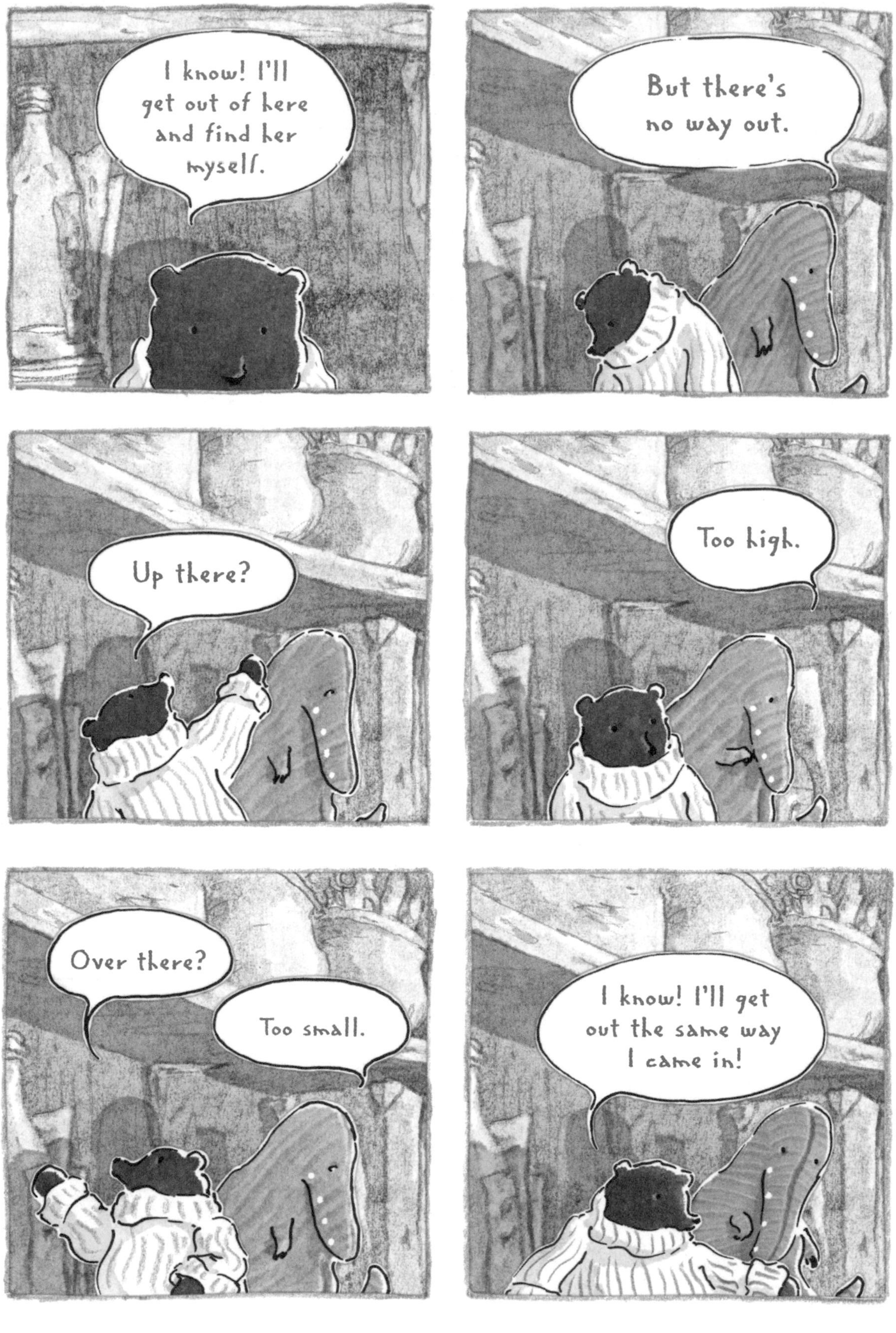
I know! I'll get out of here and find her myself.
But there's no way out.
Up there?
Too high.
Over there?
Too small.
I know! I'll get out the same way I came in!

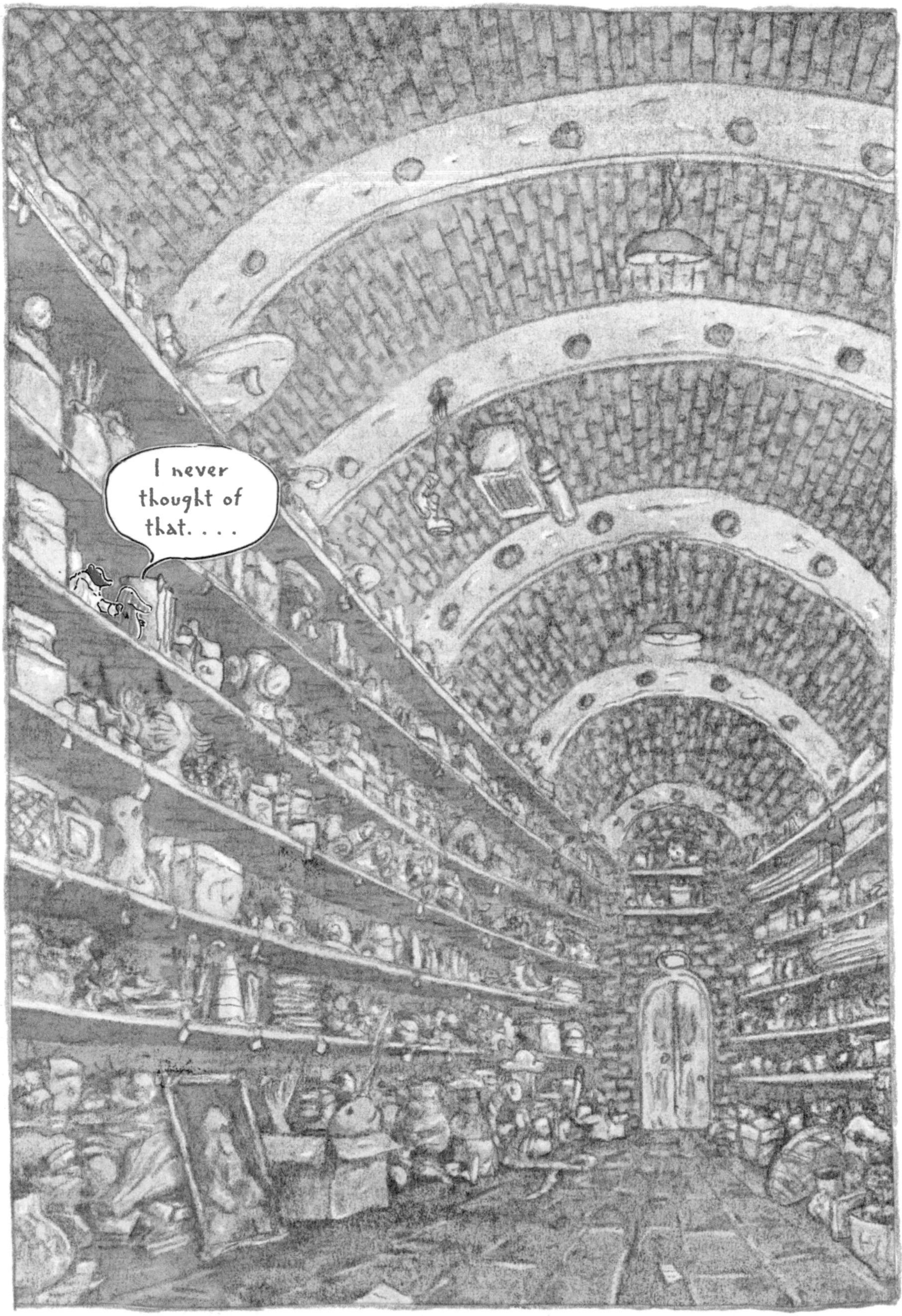
I never thought of that. . . .

The next morning, when the Man in the Hat came in, Red Ted hopped down off the shelf.

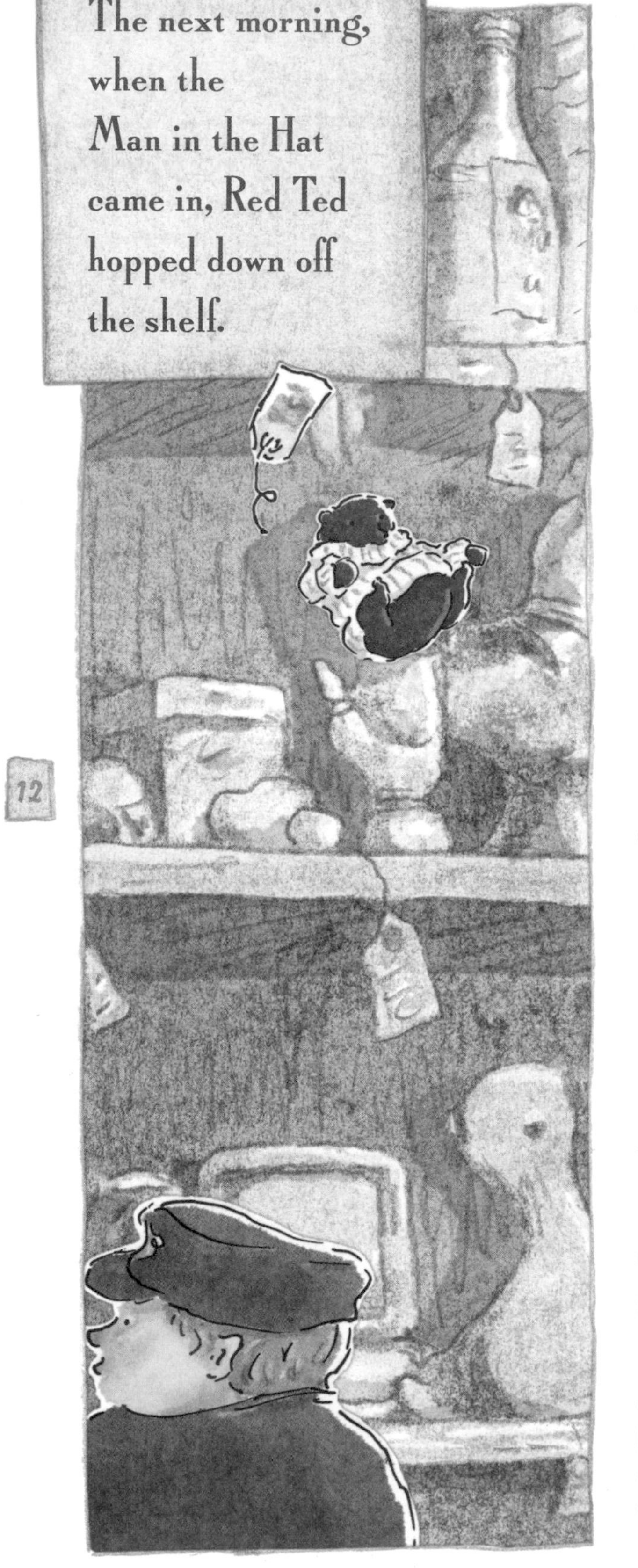

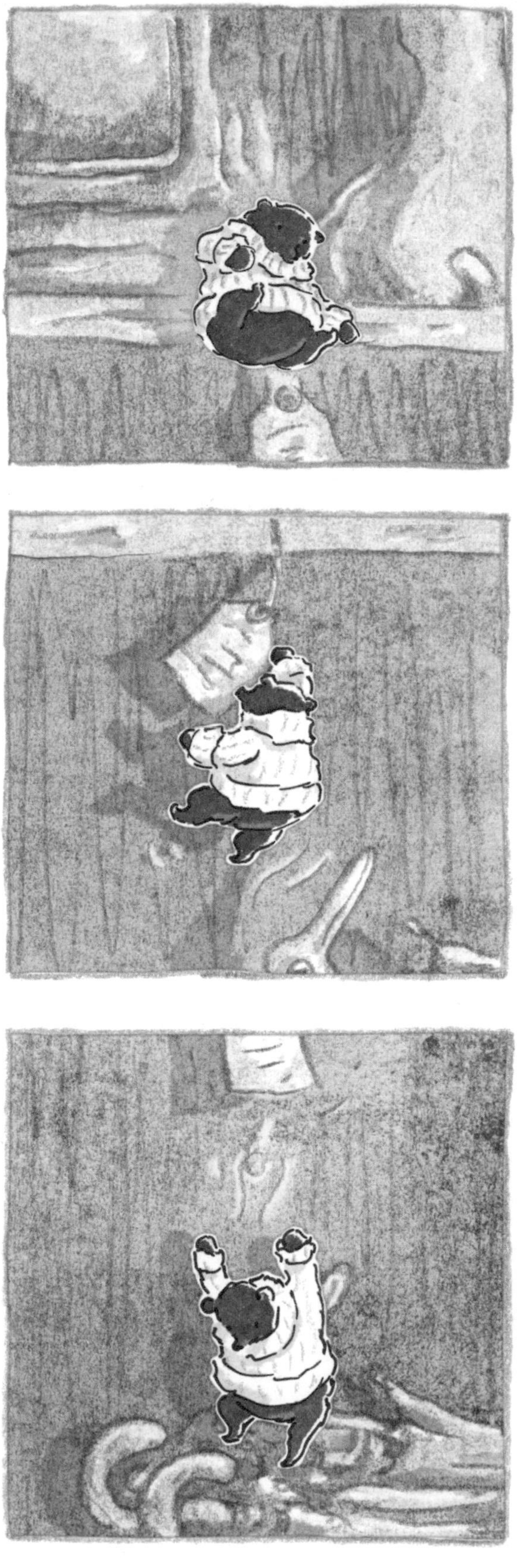

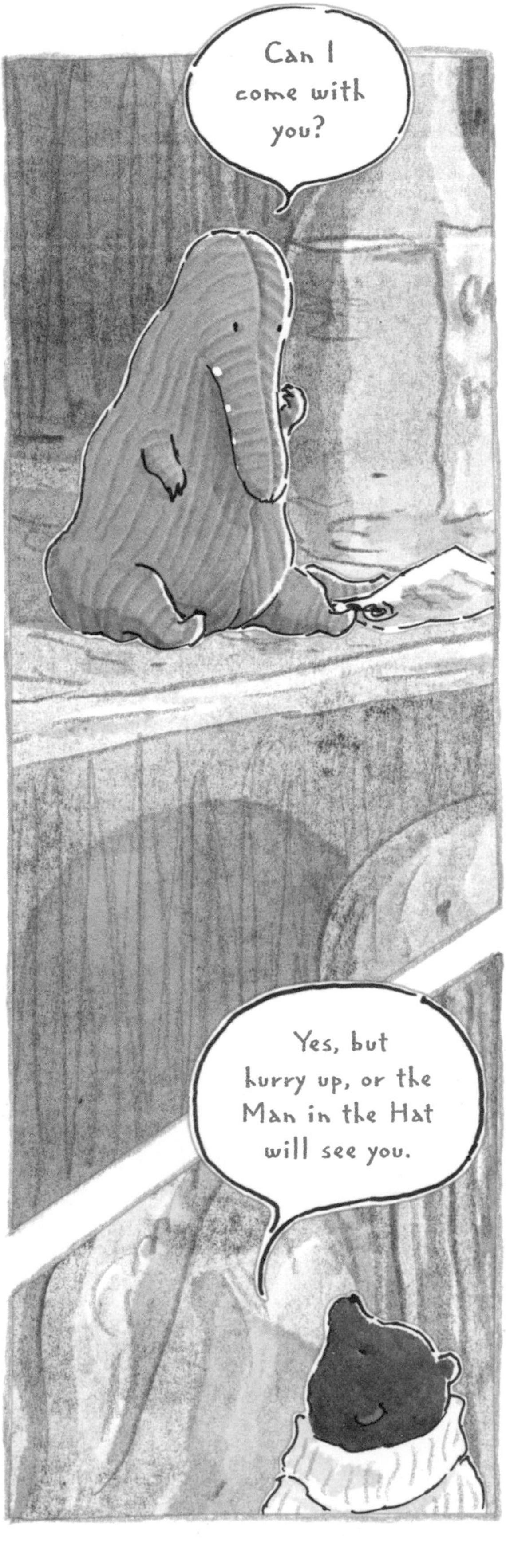
Can I come with you?
Yes, but hurry up, or the Man in the Hat will see you.

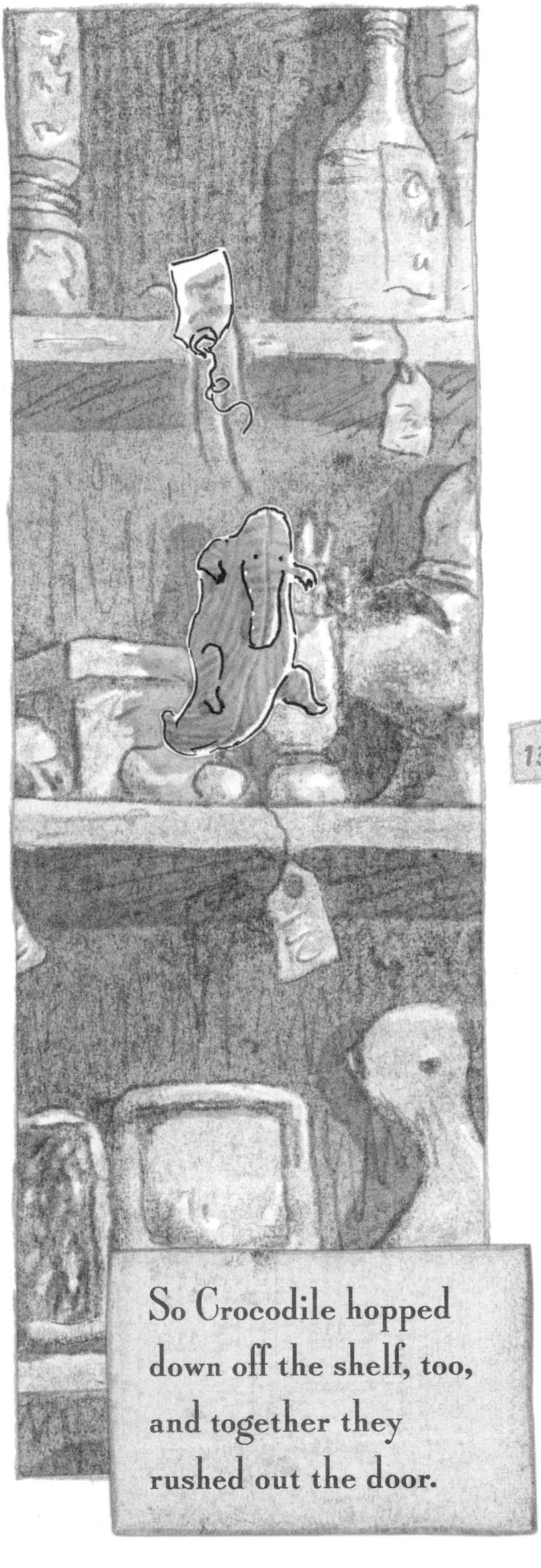
So Crocodile hopped down off the shelf, too, and together they rushed out the door.

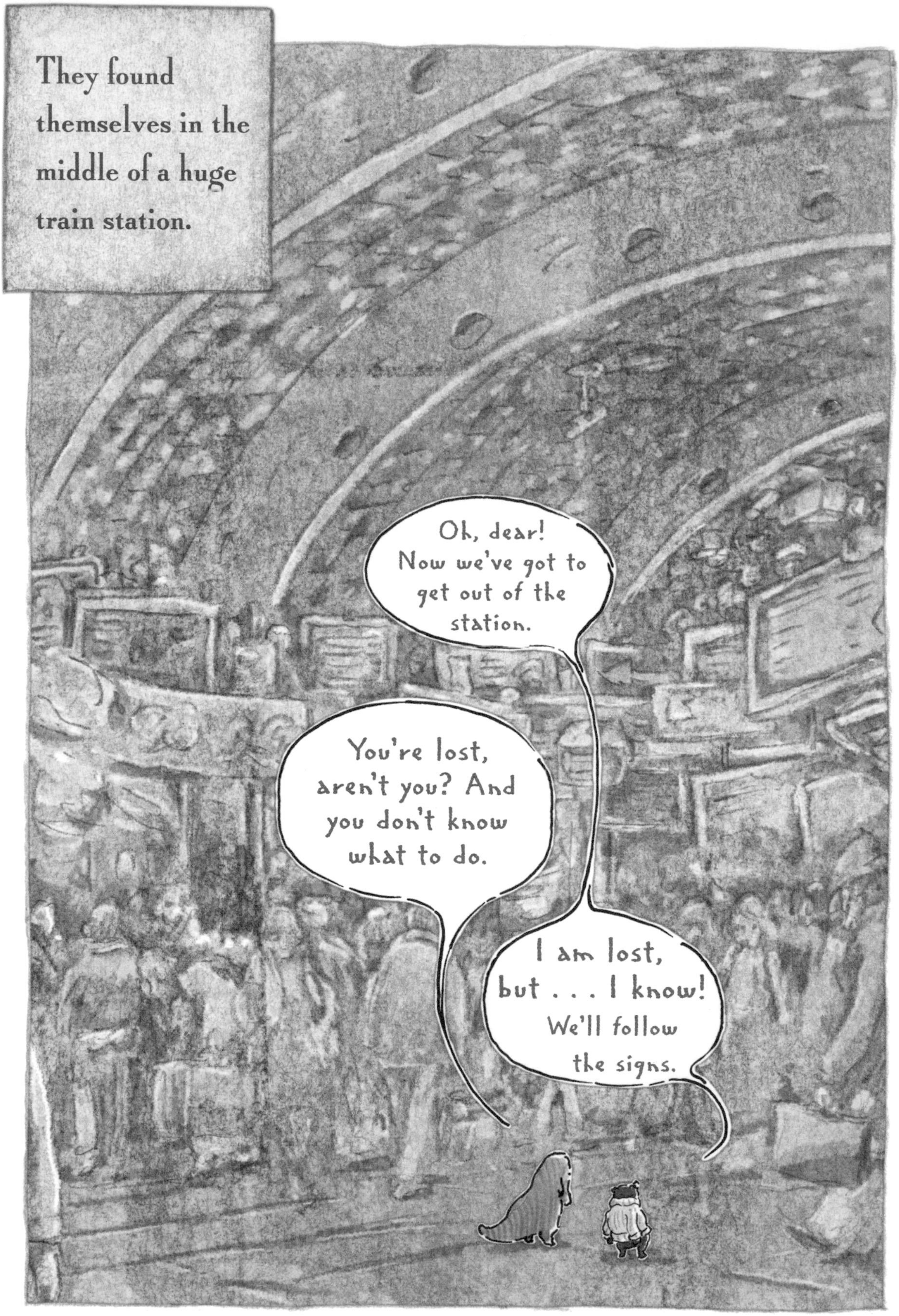
They found themselves in the middle of a huge train station.
Oh, dear! Now we've got to get out of the station.
You're lost, aren't you? And you don't know what to do.
I am lost, but . . . I know! We'll follow the signs.

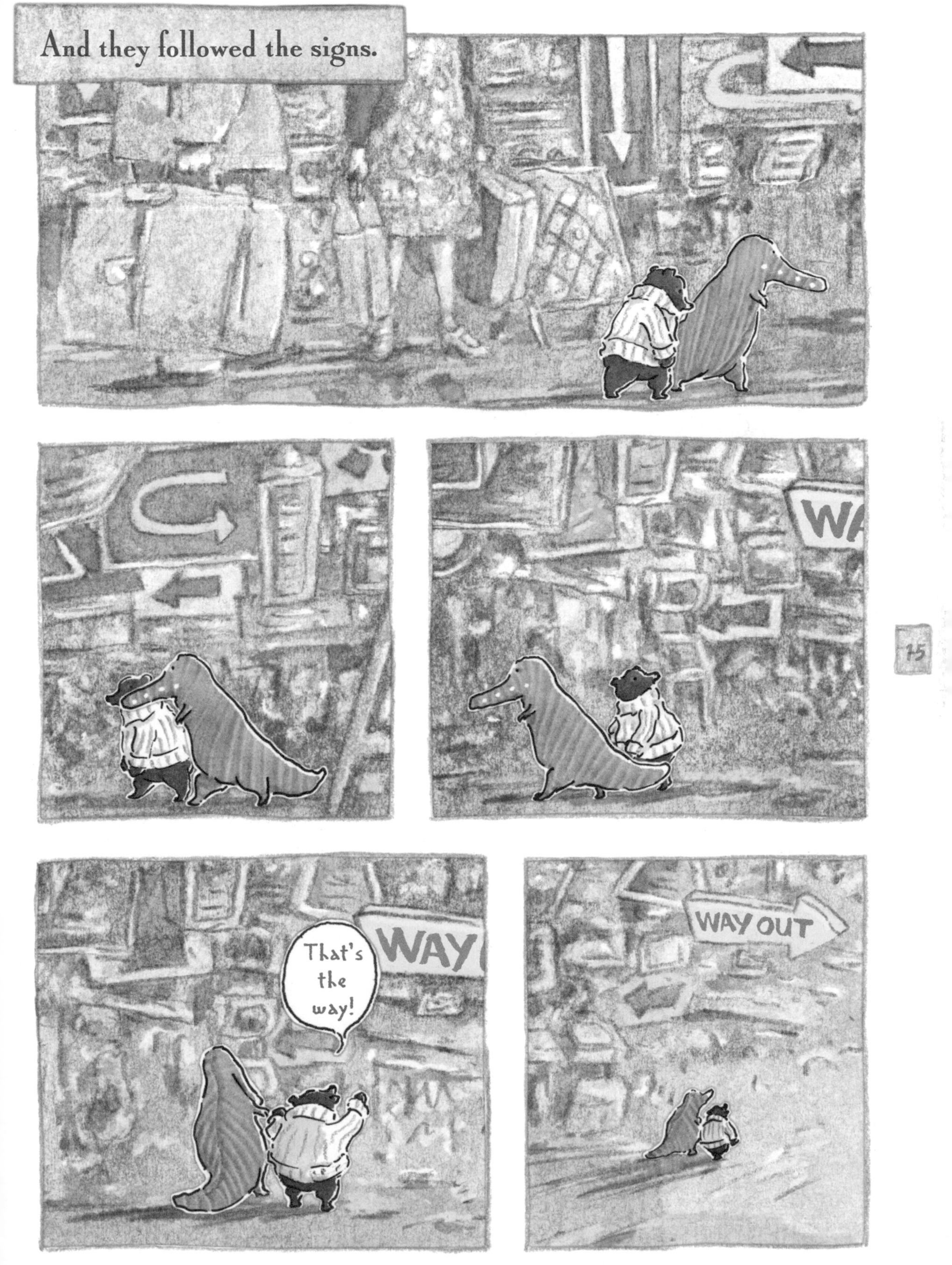
And they followed the signs.
WA
WAY
That's the way!
WAY OUT

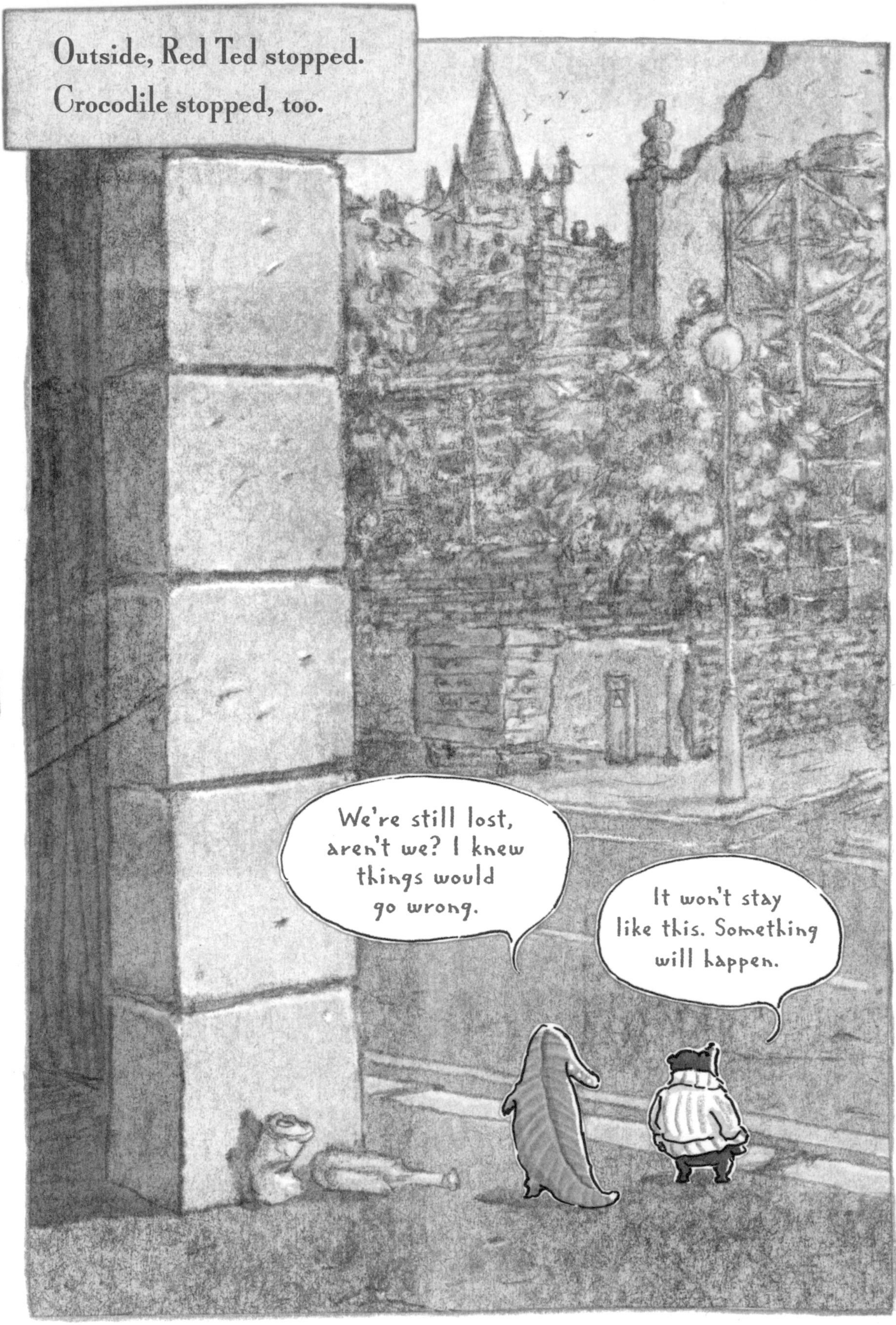
Outside, Red Ted stopped.
Crocodile stopped, too.
We're still lost, aren't we? I knew things would go wrong.
It won't stay like this. Something will happen.

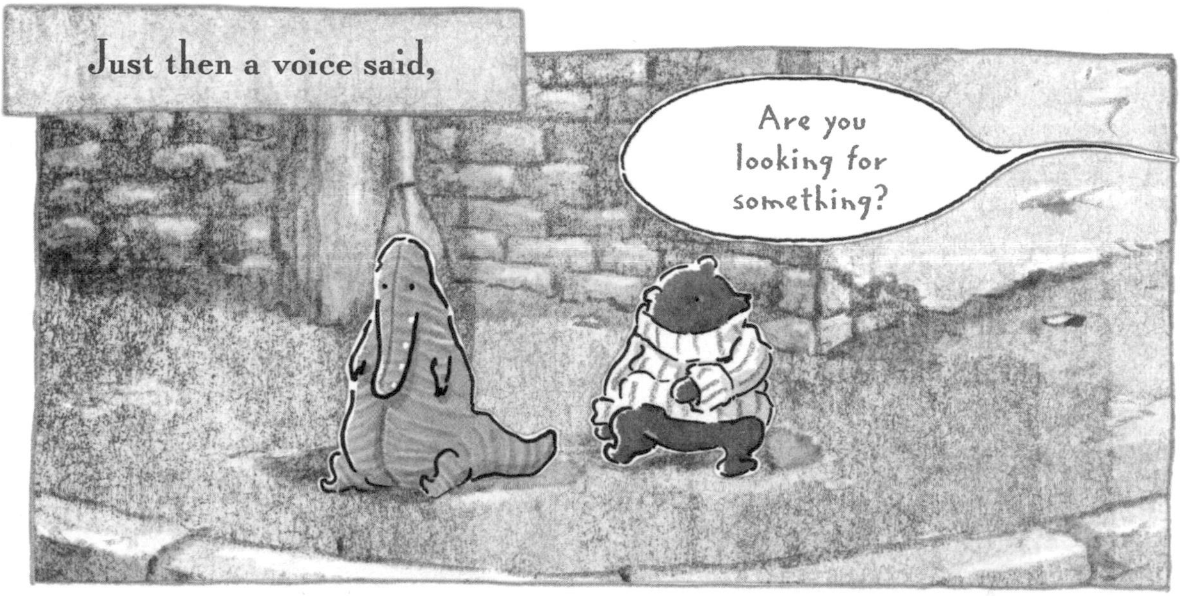
Just then a voice said,
Are you looking for something?

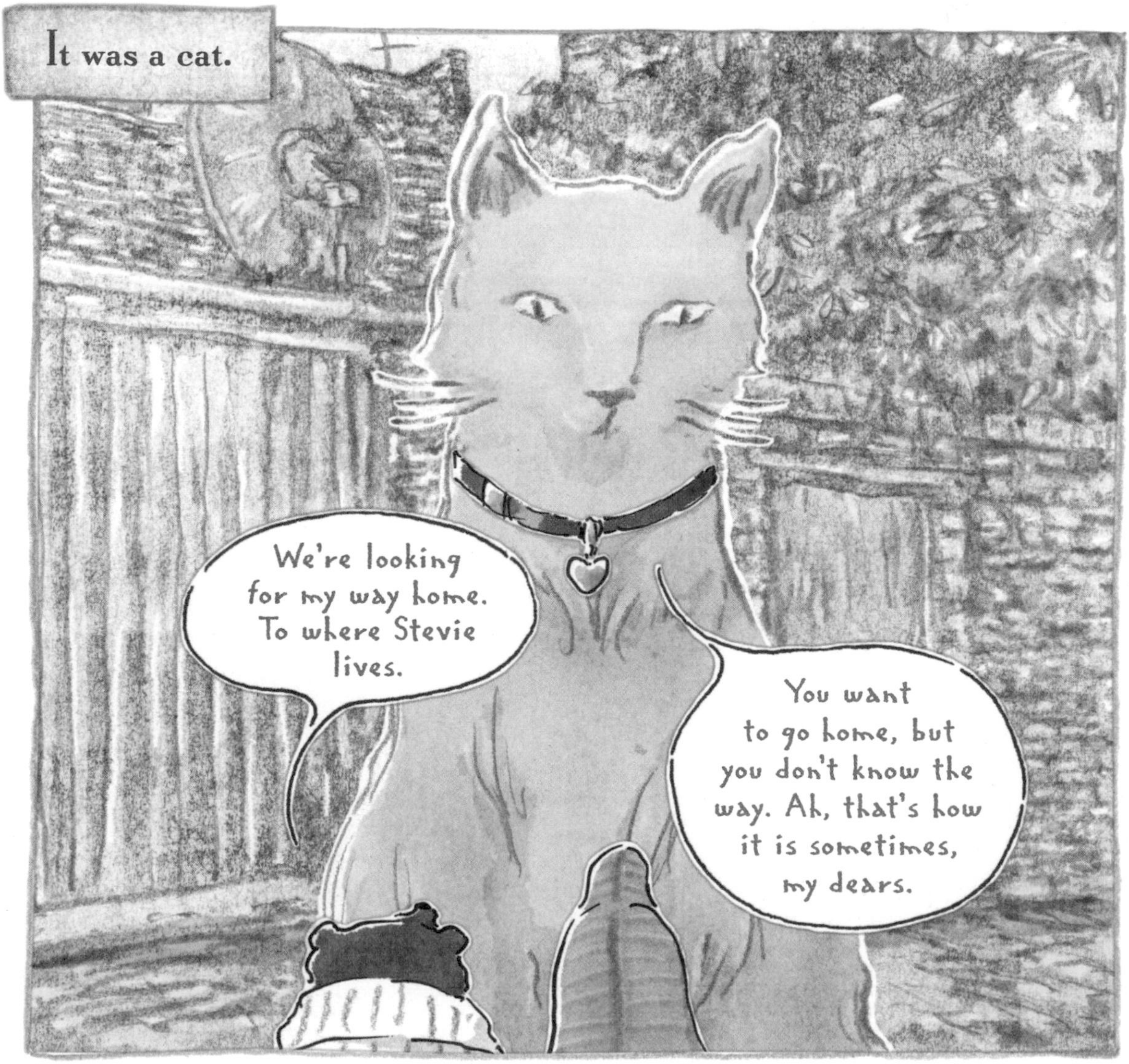
It was a cat.
We're looking for my way home. To where Stevie lives.
You want to go home, but you don't know the way. Ah, that's how it is sometimes, my dears.

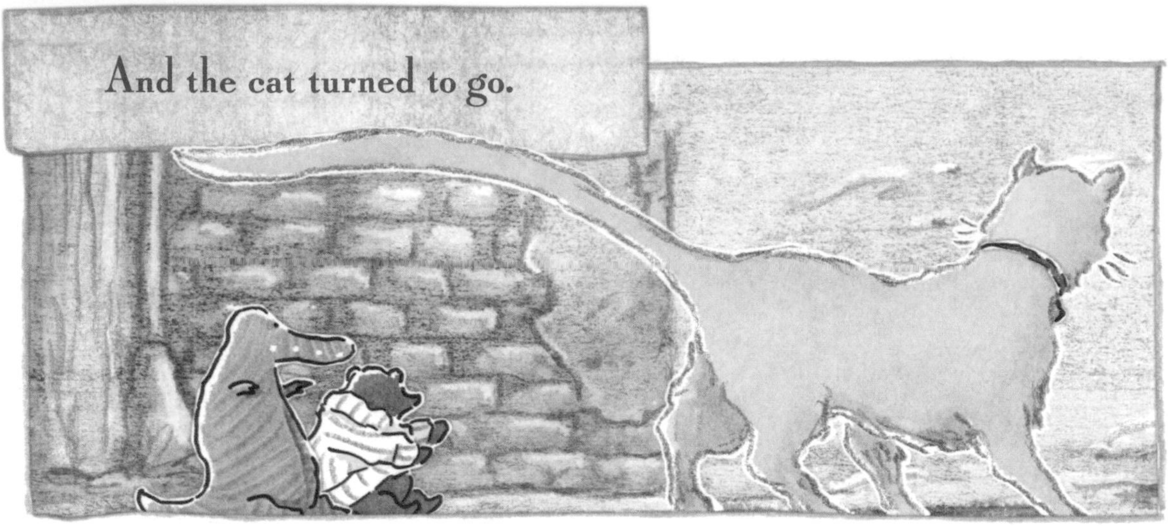
And the cat turned to go.

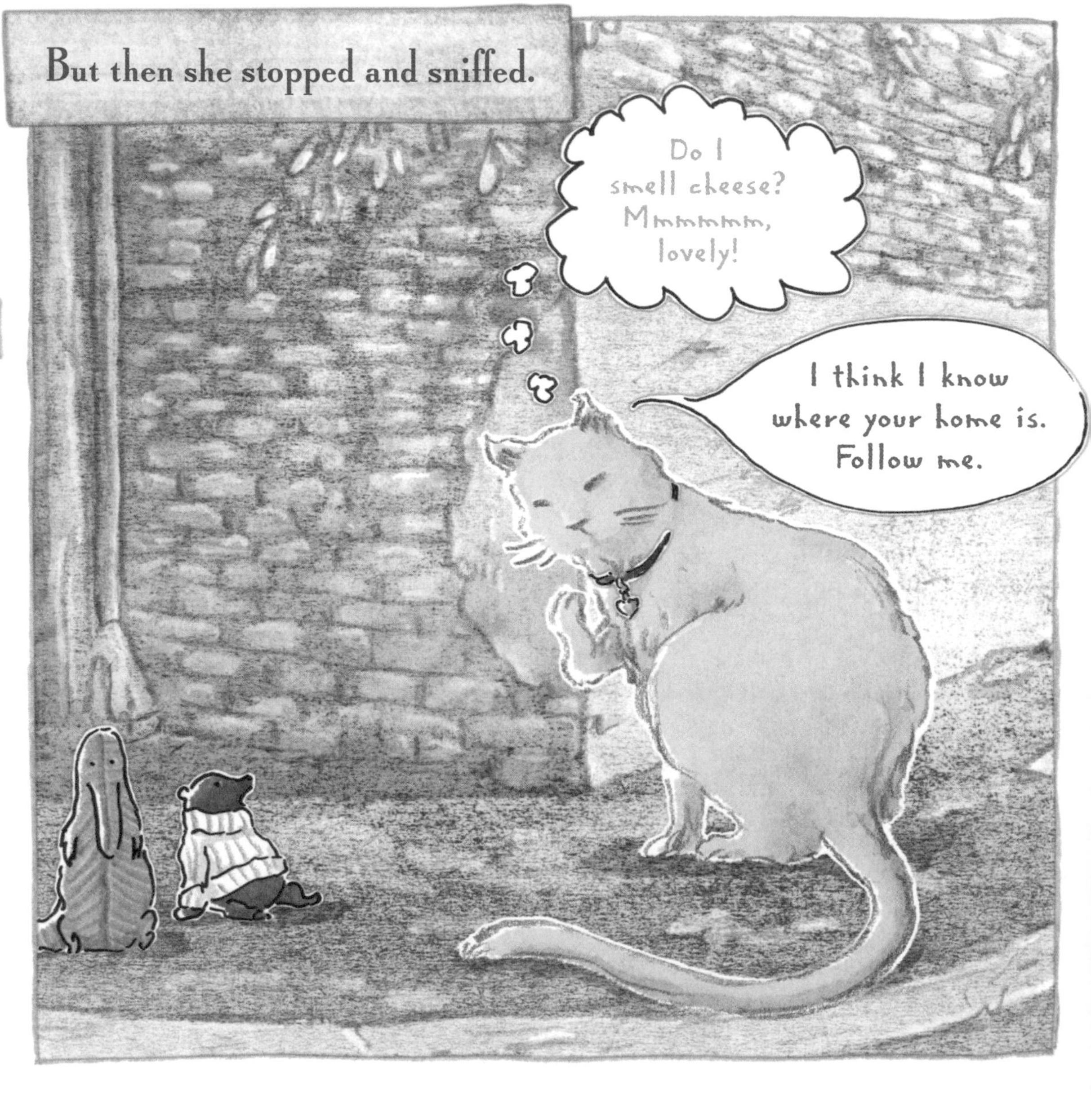
But then she stopped and sniffed.
Do I smell cheese? Mmmmmm, lovely!
I think I know where your home is. Follow me.

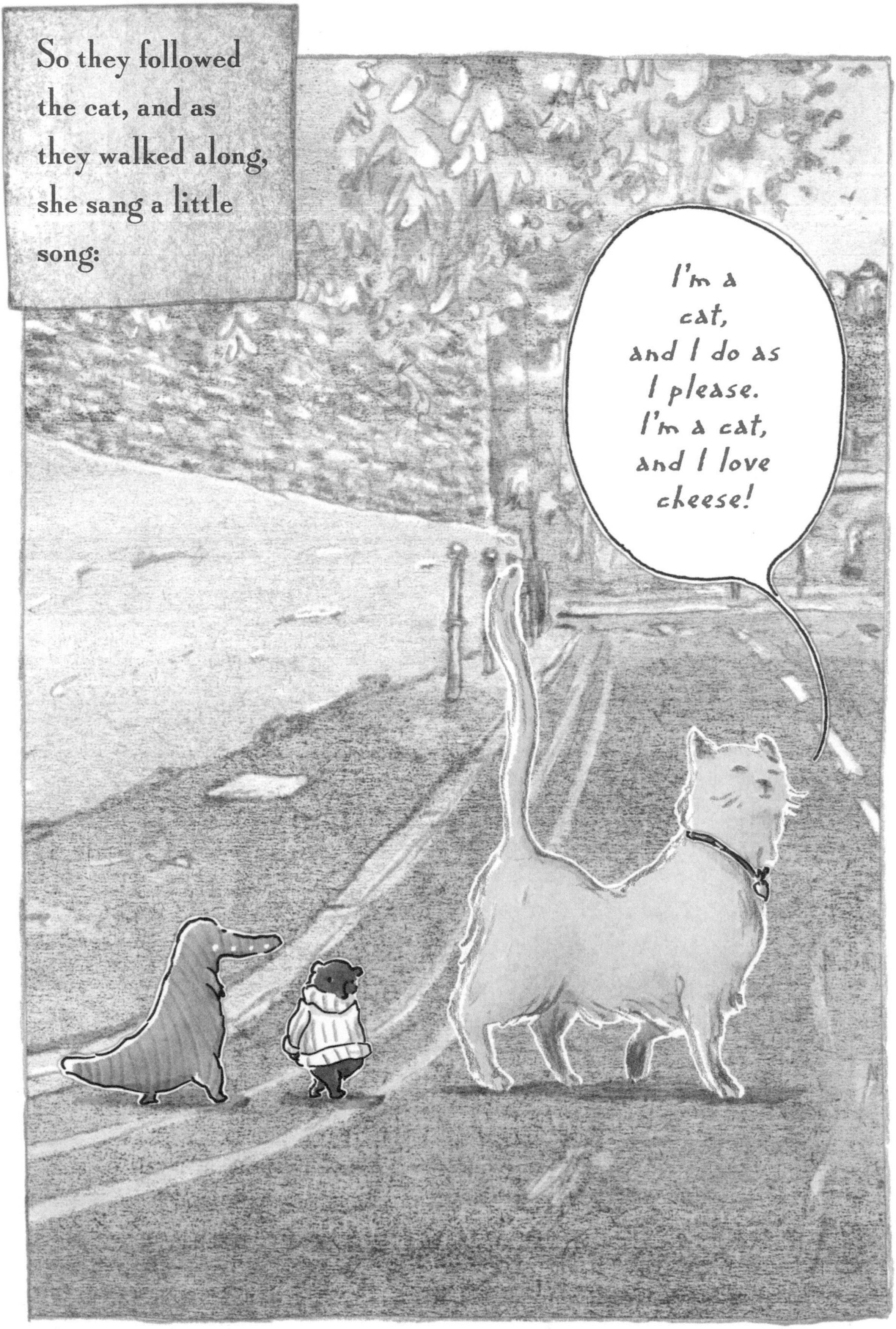
So they followed the cat, and as they walked along, she sang a little song:
I'm a cat, and I do as I please. I'm a cat, and I love cheese!

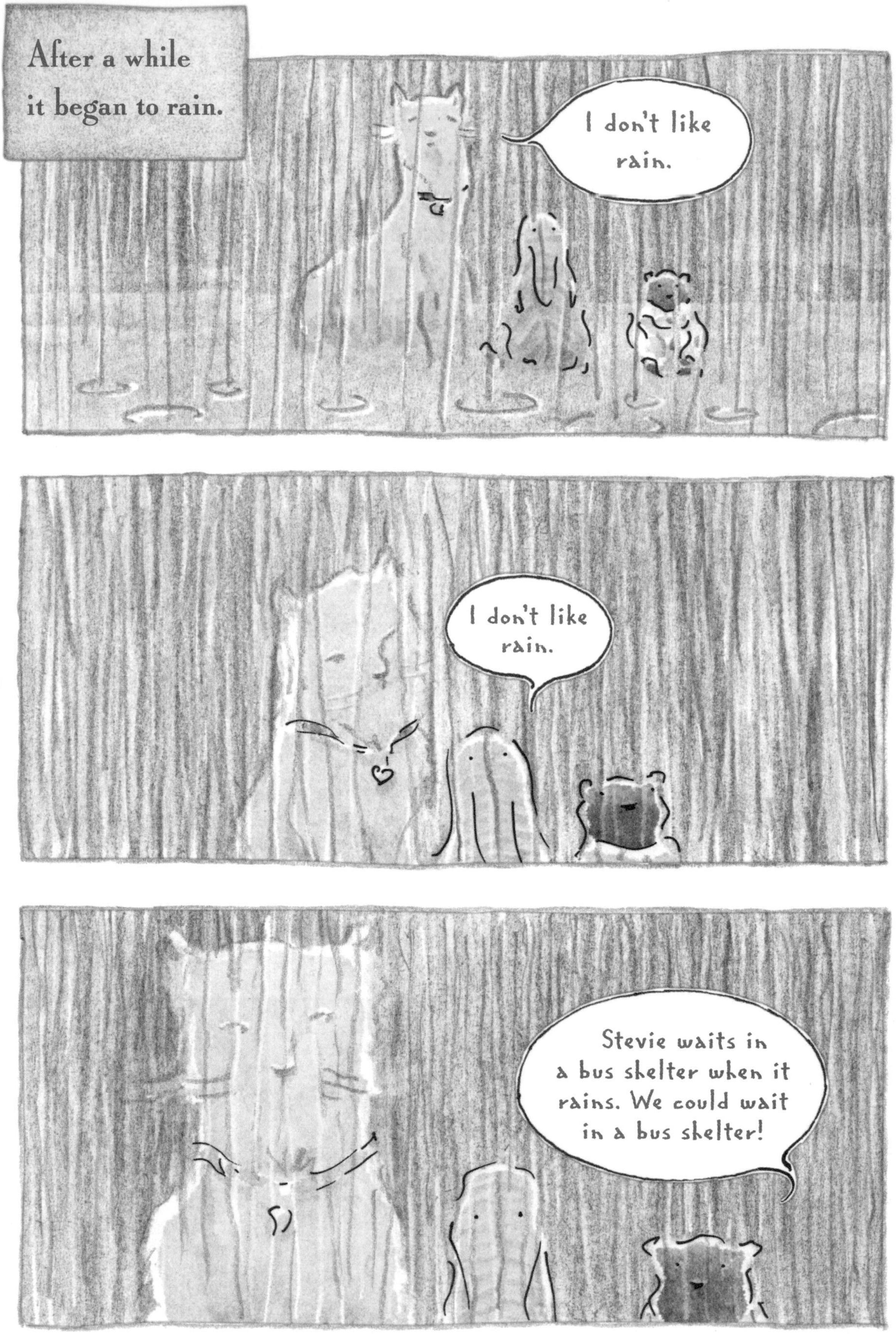
After a while it began to rain.
I don't like rain.
I don't like rain.
Stevie waits in a bus shelter when it rains. We could wait in a bus shelter!

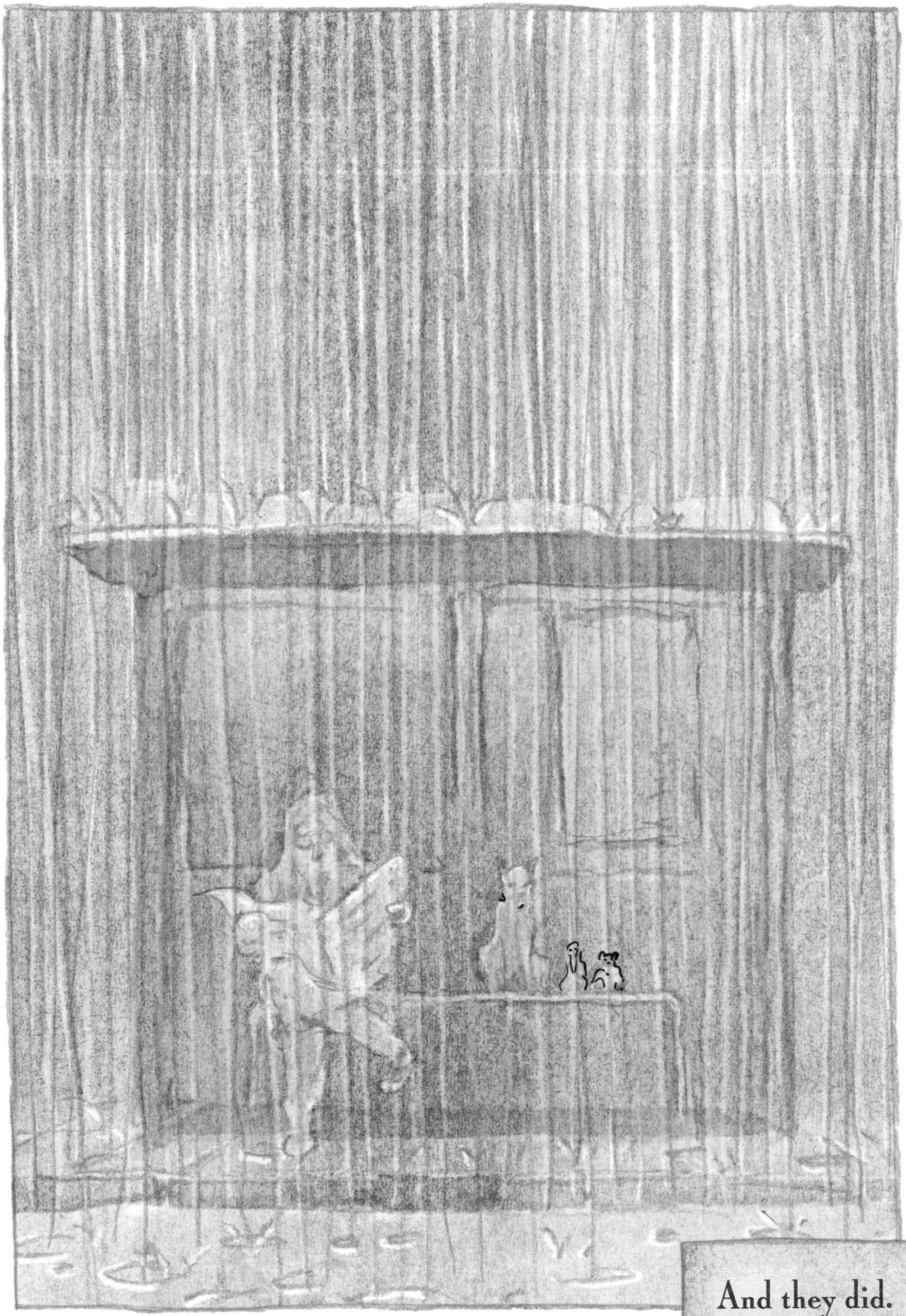

And they did.

When the rain stopped,
they walked on—
through the market,
under a bridge,
down an alley.

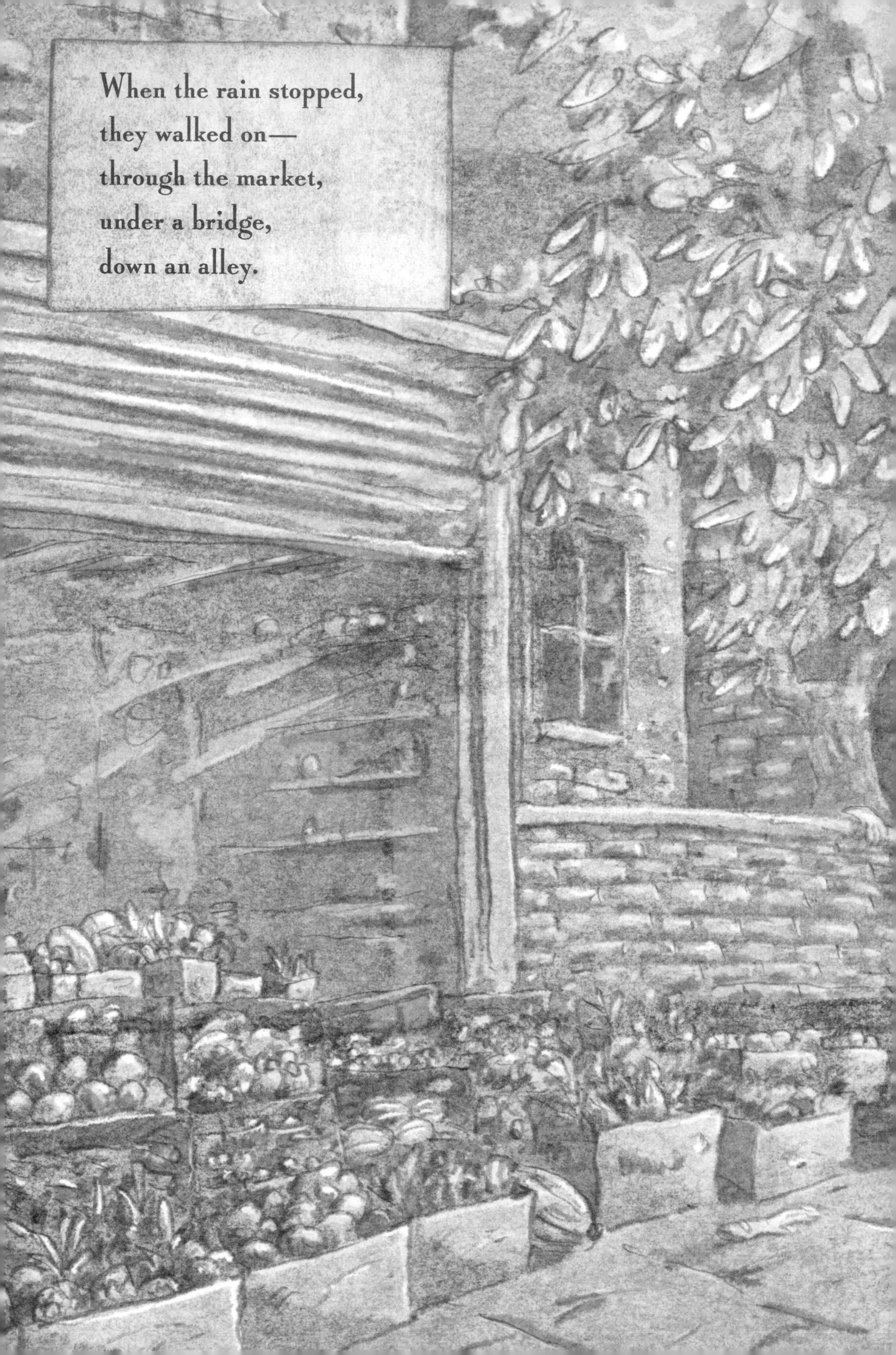

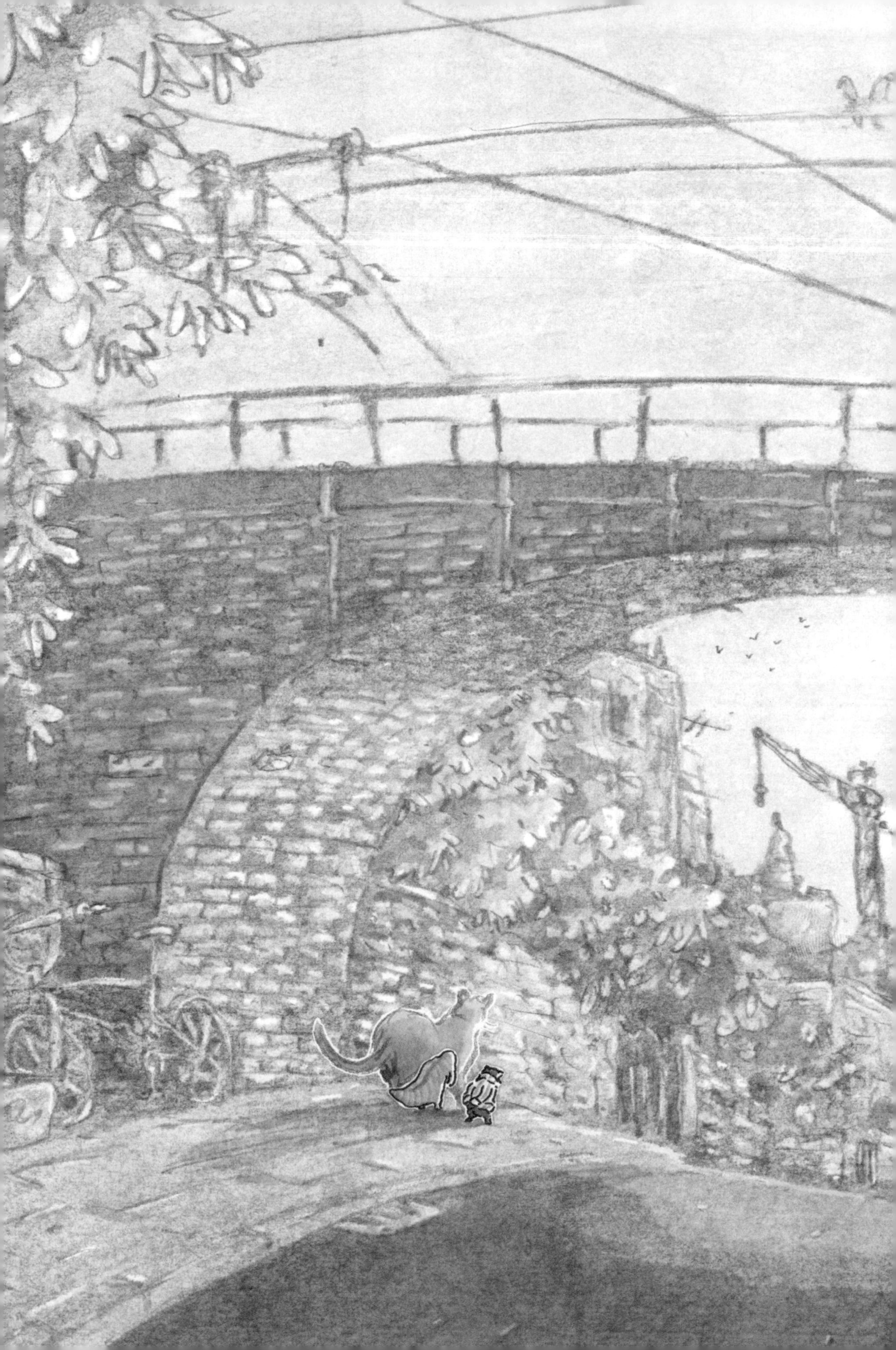

Suddenly a great big dog — a huge, enormous giant of a dog — jumped out at them. He stood in their way and growled.

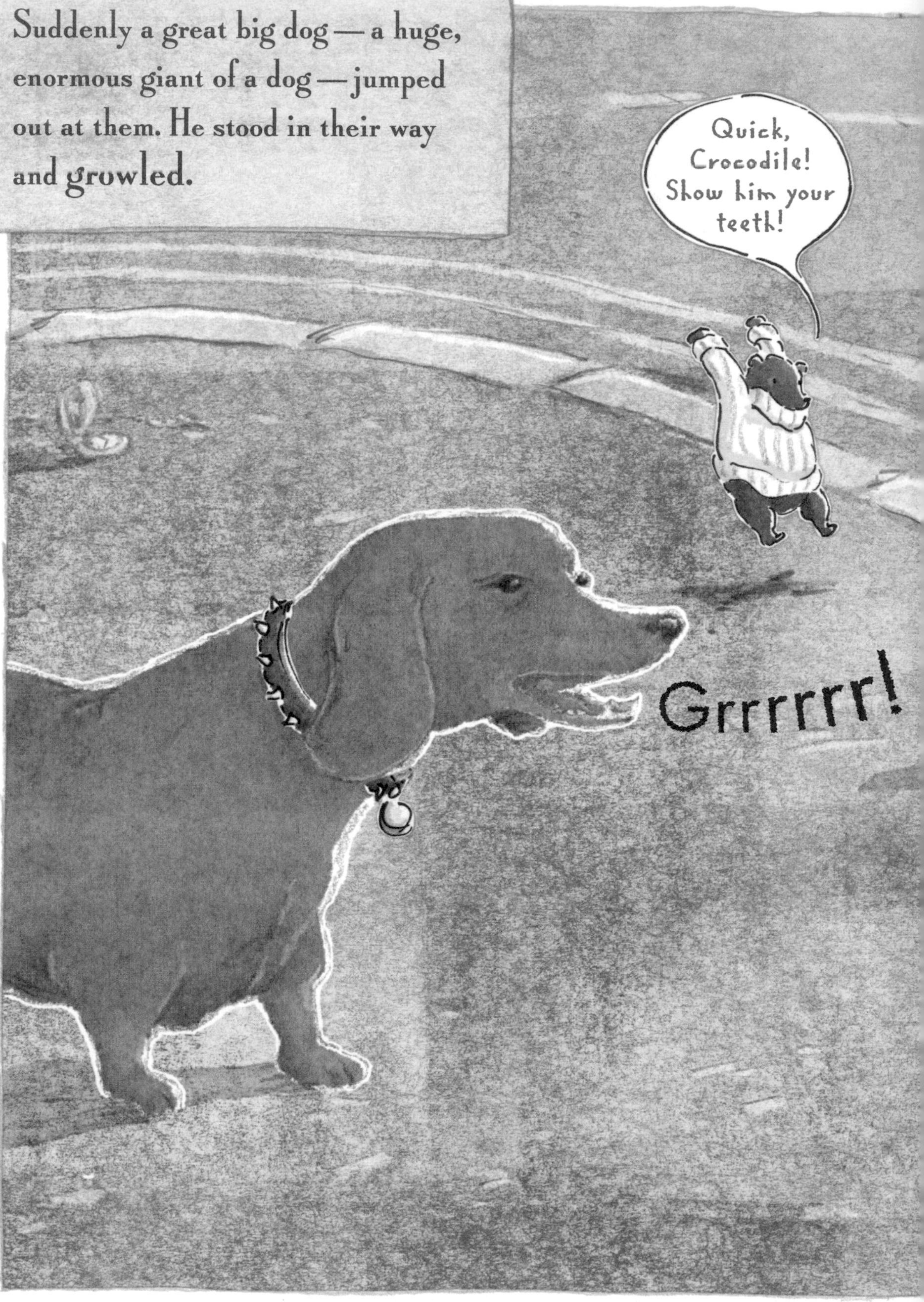
Quick, Crocodile! Show him your teeth!
Grrrrrr!

25

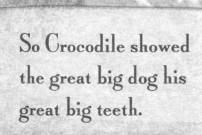

So Crocodile showed the great big dog his great big teeth.

The great big dog didn't like Crocodile's great big teeth, and it ran away.

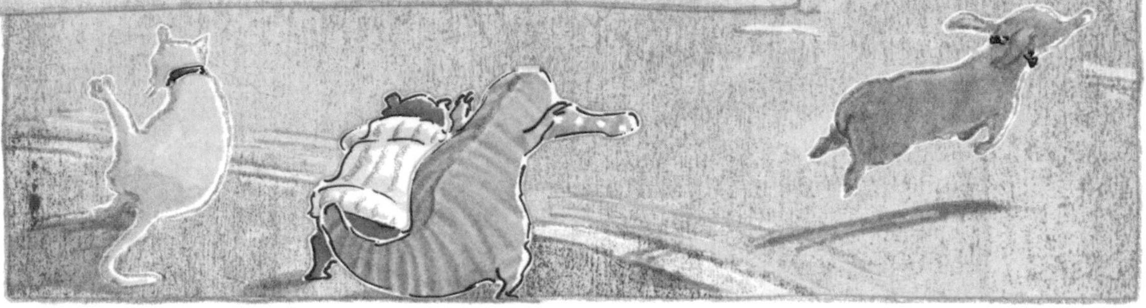

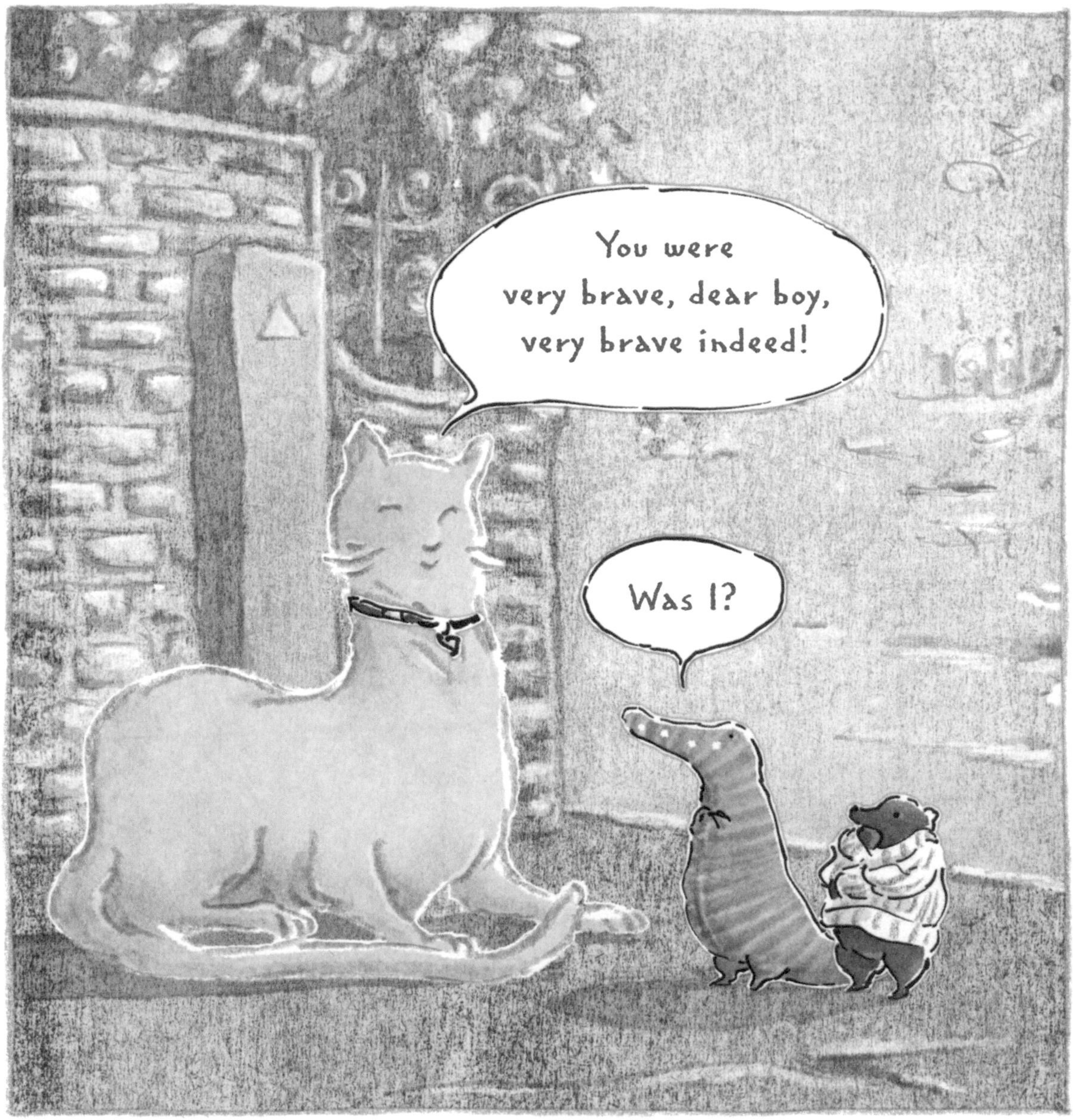
You were very brave, dear boy, very brave indeed!
Was I?

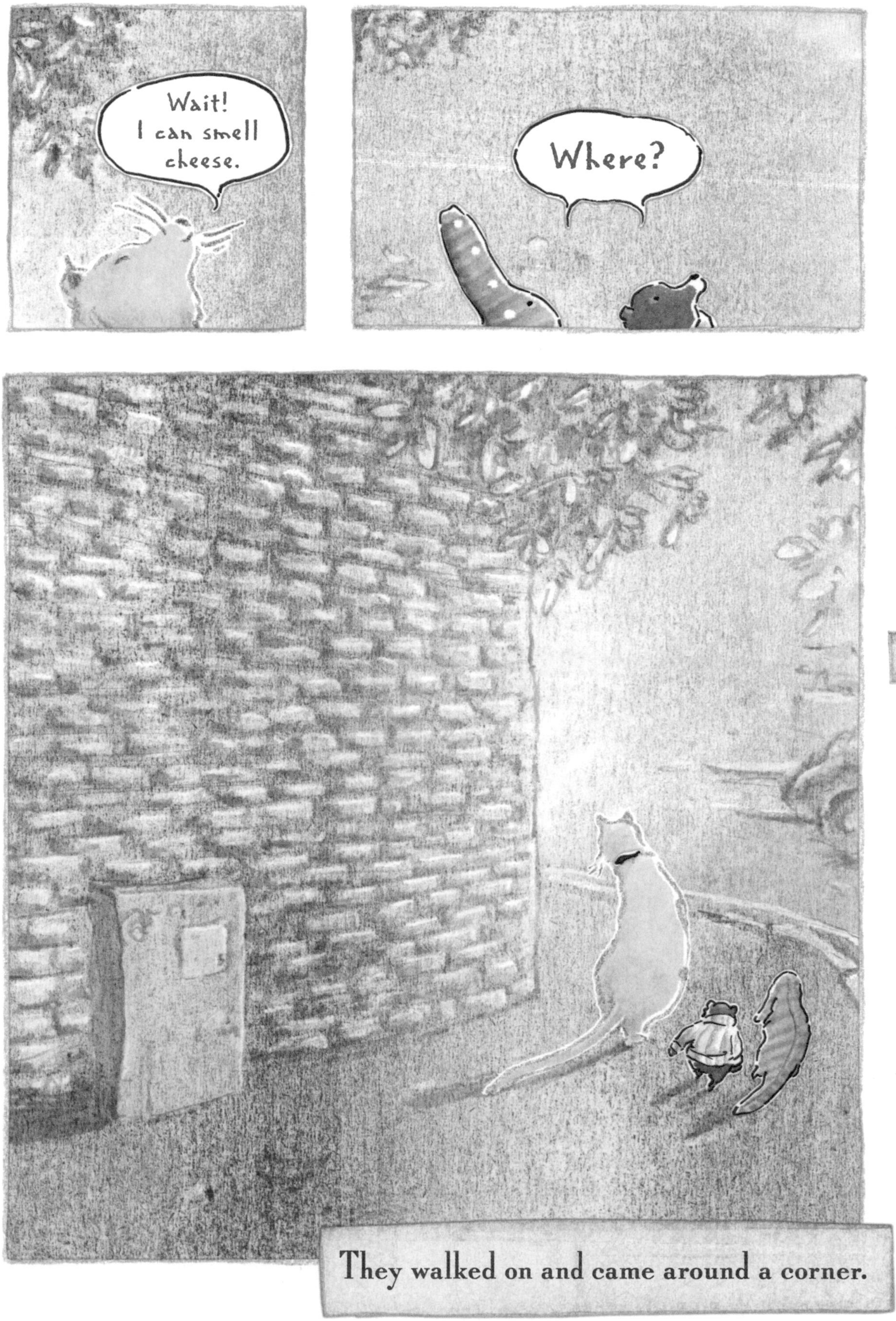
Wait! I can smell cheese.
Where?
They walked on and came around a corner.

Red Ted stopped.

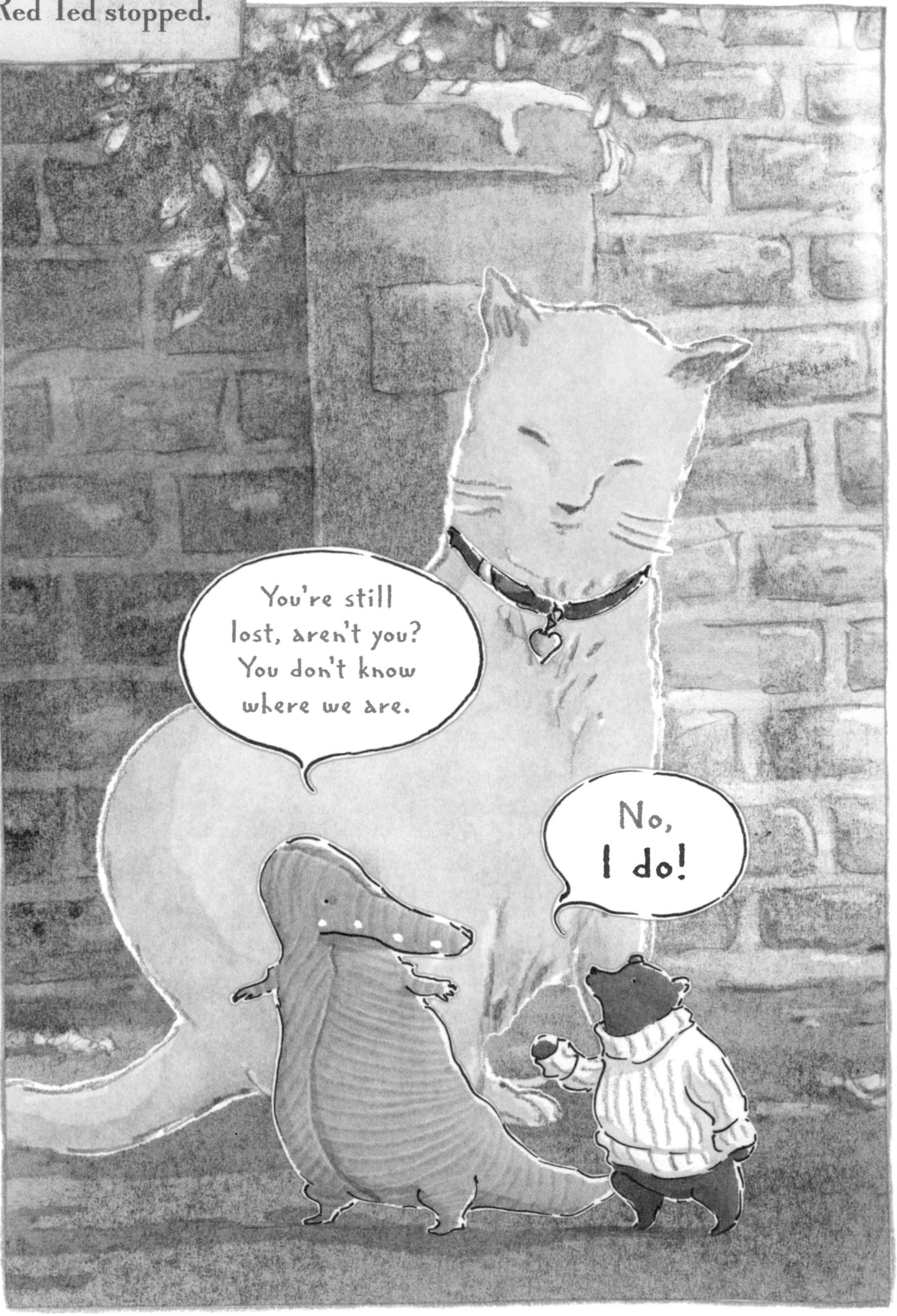
You're still lost, aren't you? You don't know where we are.
No, I do!

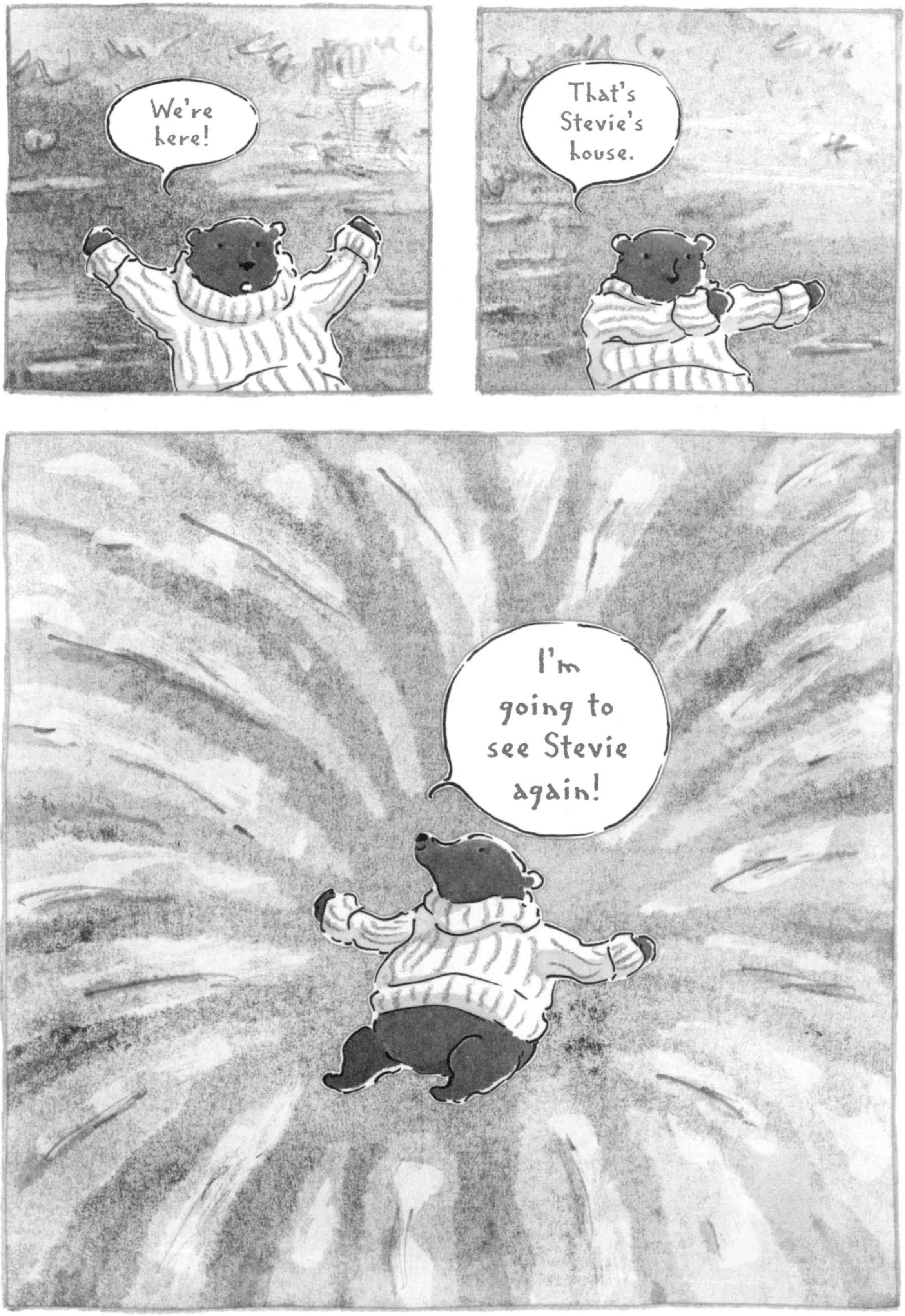
We're here!
That's Stevie's house.
I'm going to see Stevie again!

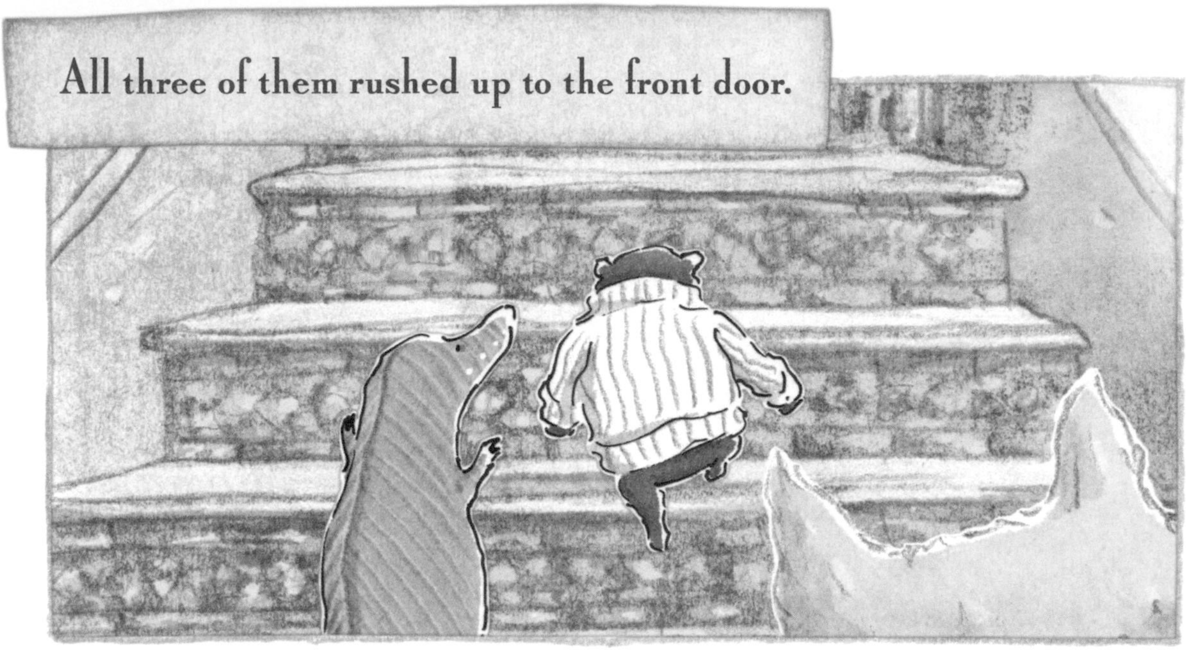
All three of them rushed up to the front door.

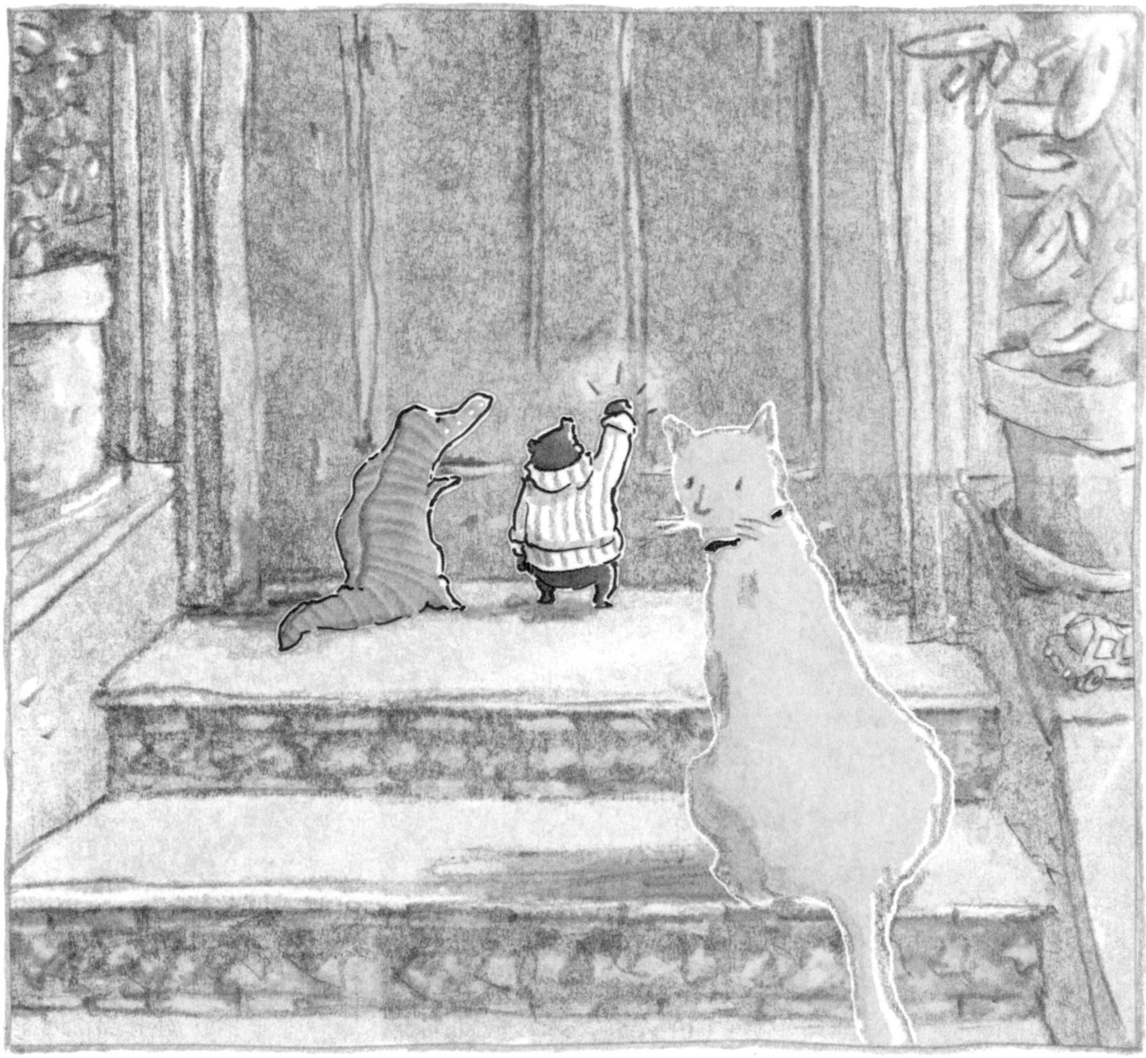

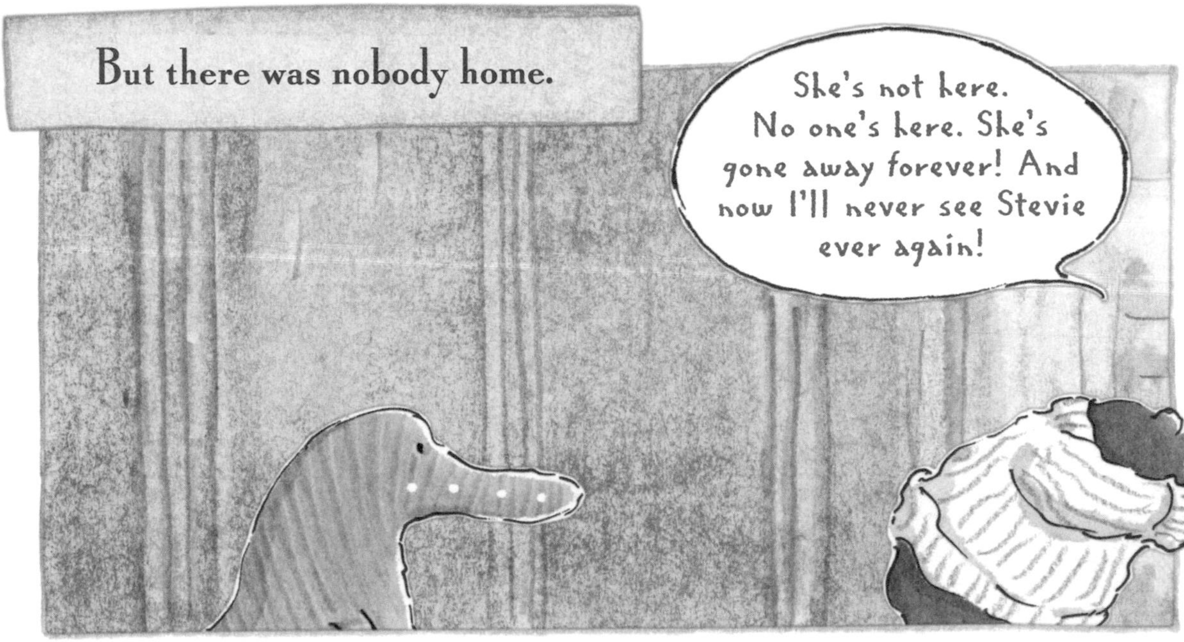
But there was nobody home.
She's not here. No one's here. She's gone away forever! And now I'll never see Stevie ever again!

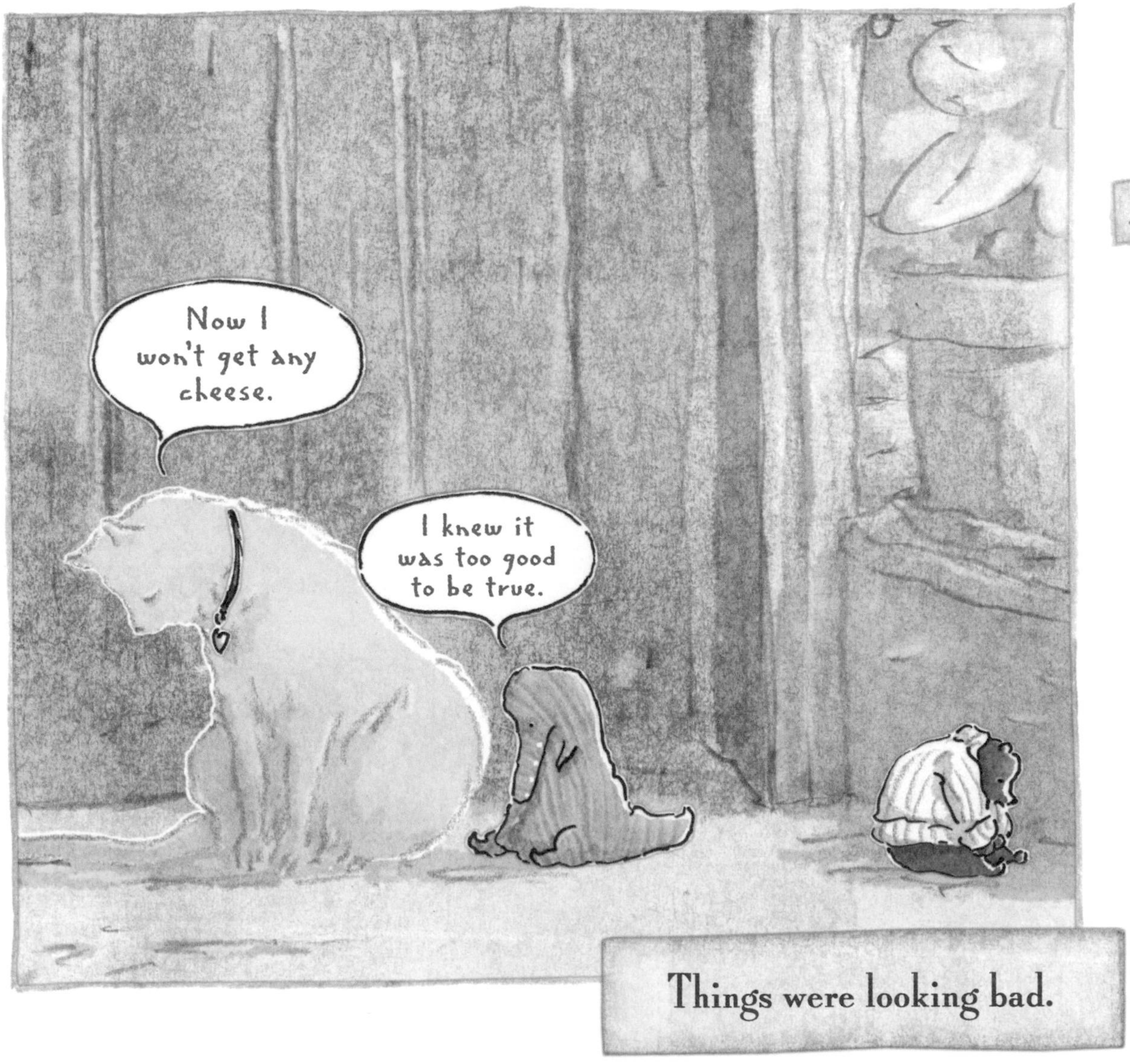
Now I won't get any cheese.
I knew it was too good to be true.
Things were looking bad.

Then, suddenly, around the corner, came . . . Stevie!

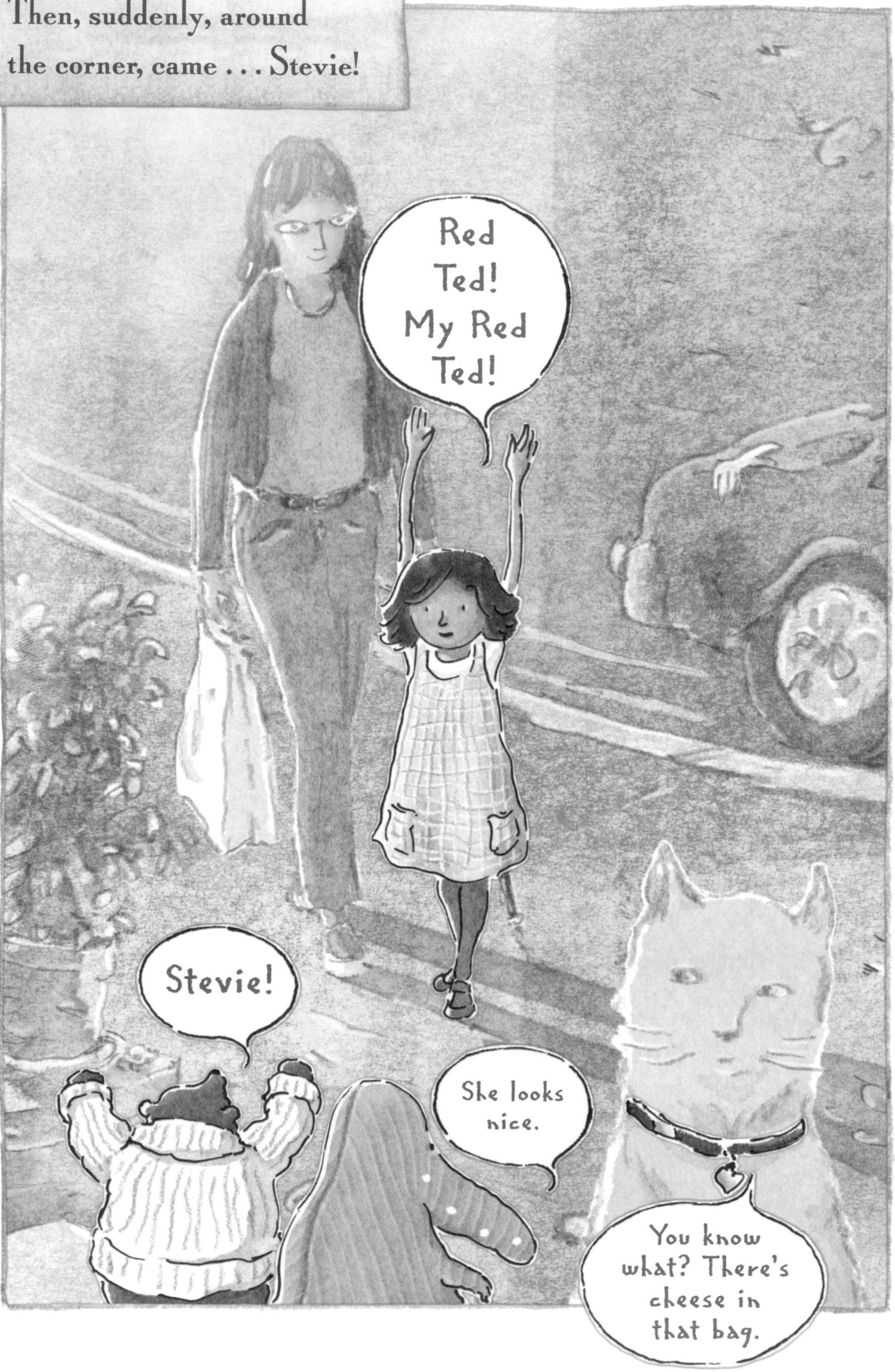

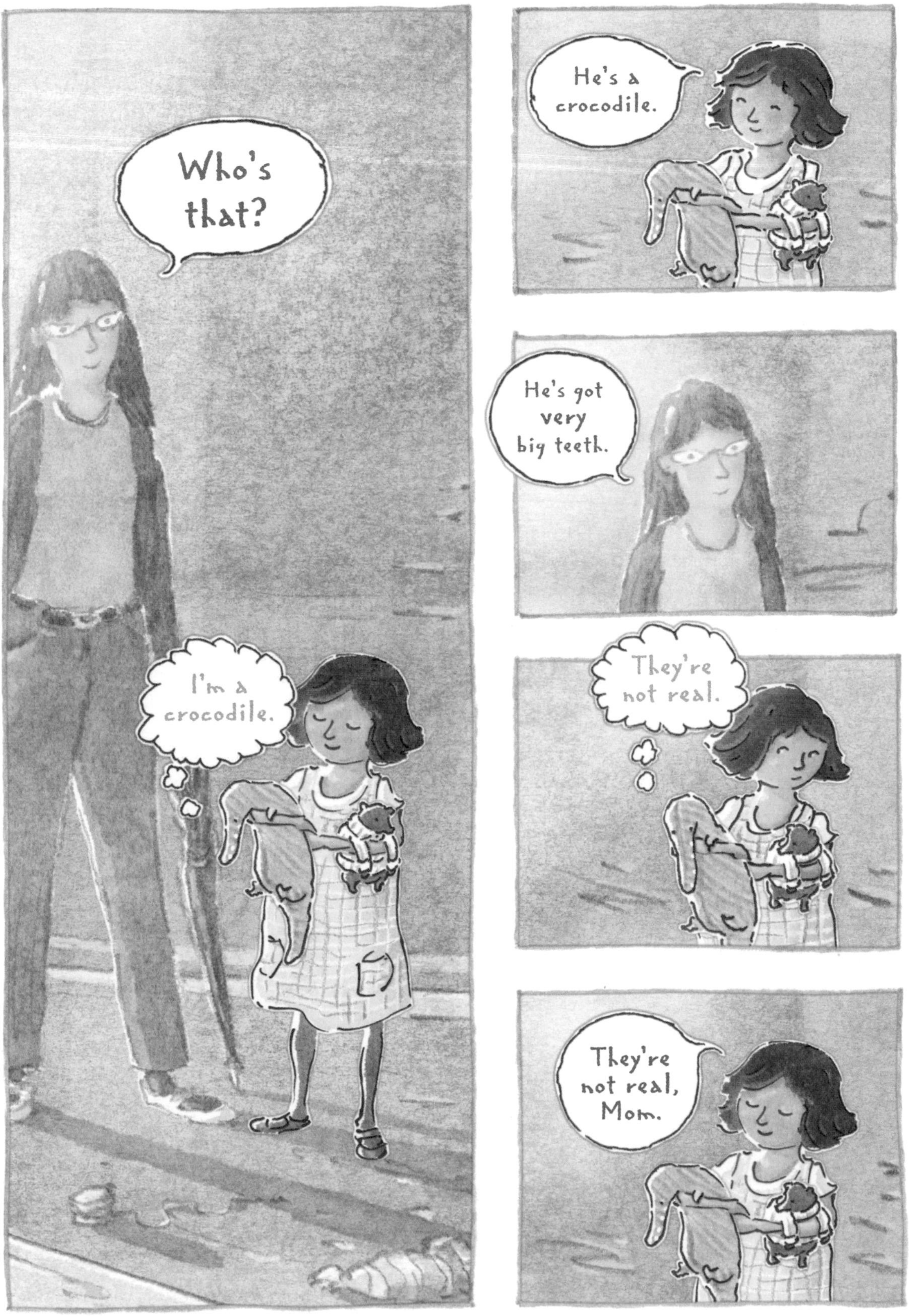
Who's that?
I'm a crocodile.
He's a crocodile.
He's got very big teeth.
They're not real.
They're not real, Mom.

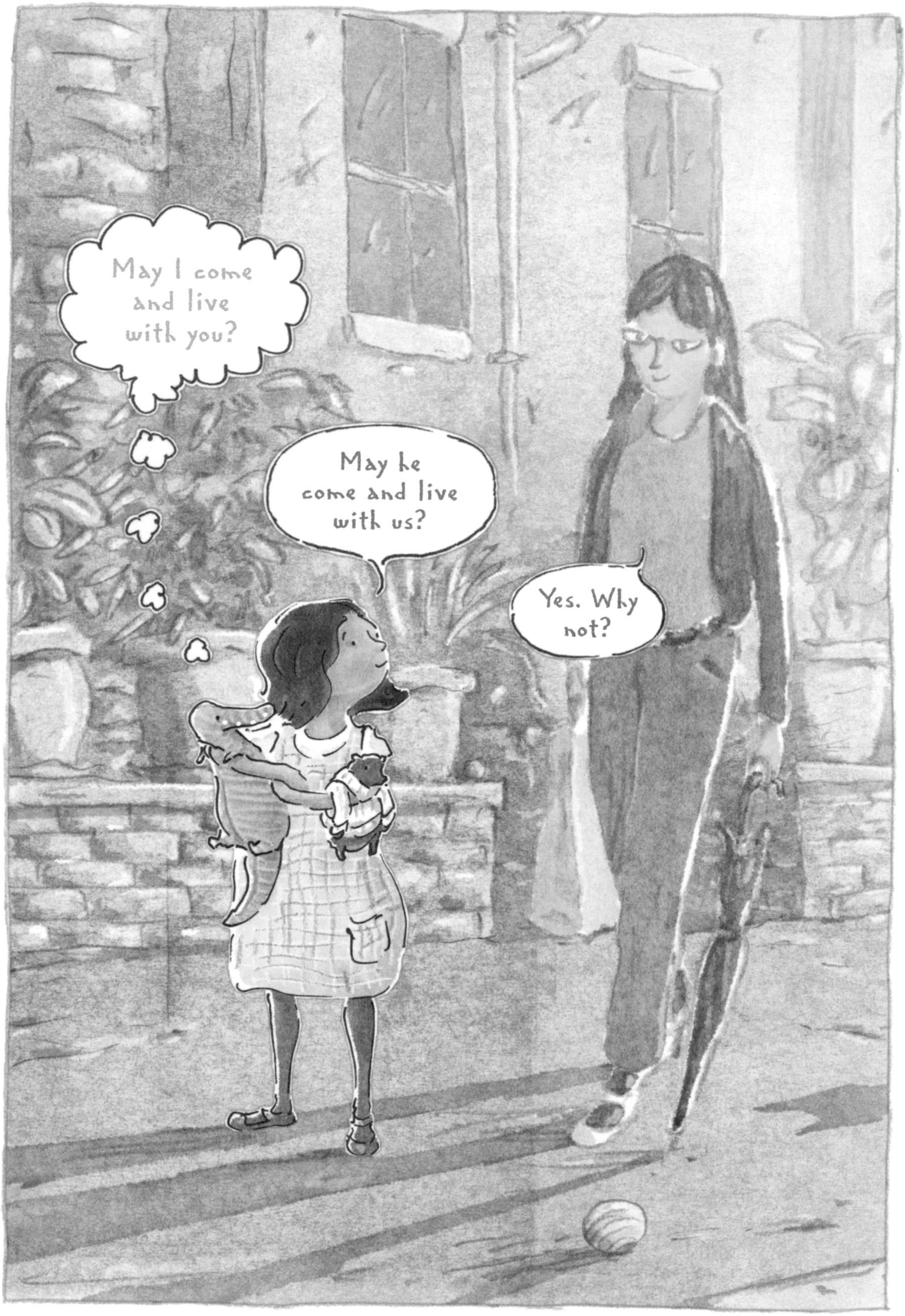
May I come and live with you?
May he come and live with us?
Yes. Why not?

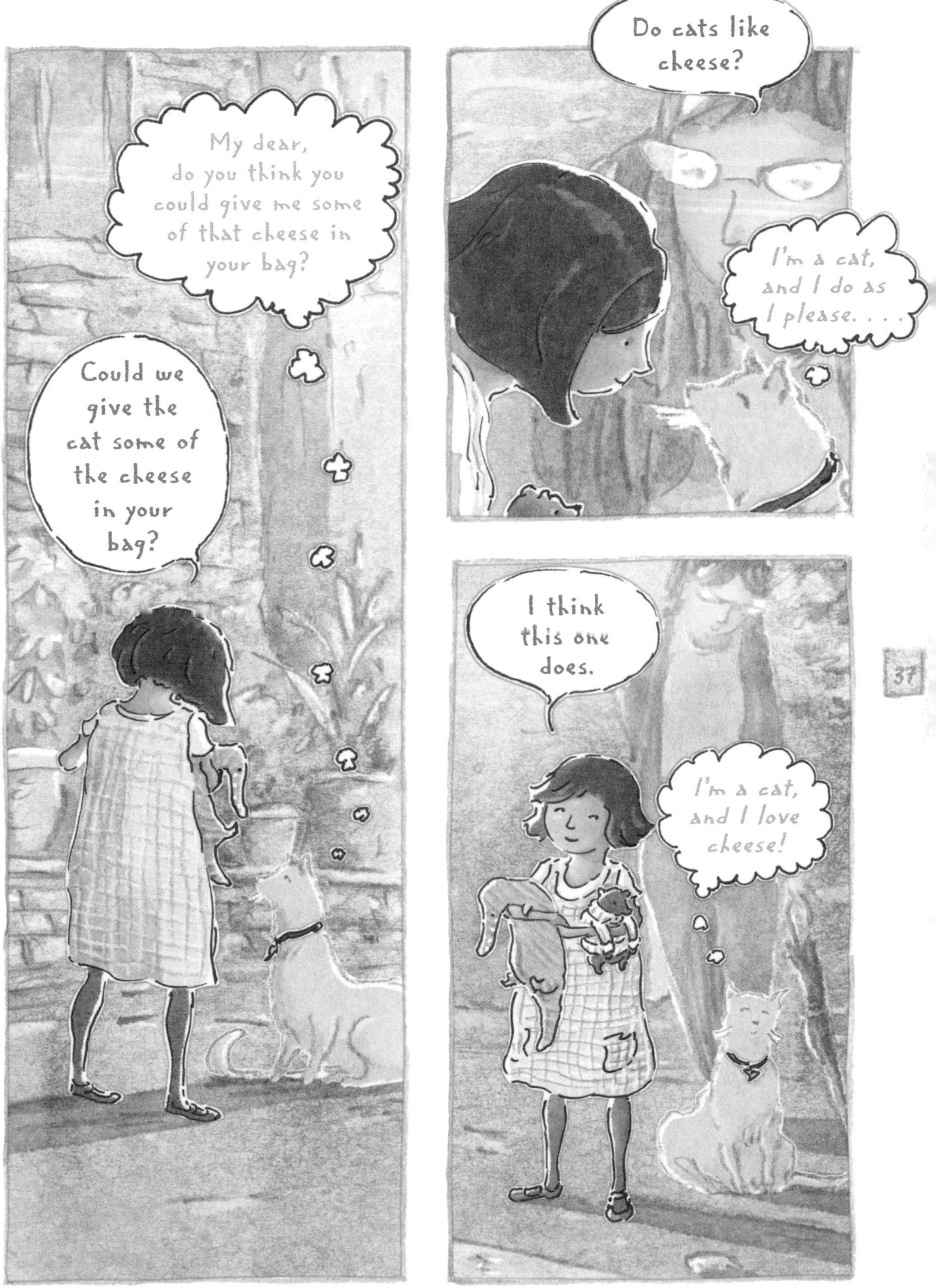
My dear, do you think you could give me some of that cheese in your bag?
Could we give the cat some of the cheese in your bag?
Do cats like cheese?
I'm a cat, and I do as I please. . . .
I think this one does.
I'm a cat, and I love cheese!

That night when Stevie went to bed, she was happy. Crocodile was happy. The cat was happy. But no one was happier than Red Ted, who'd found Stevie again and wasn't lost anymore.

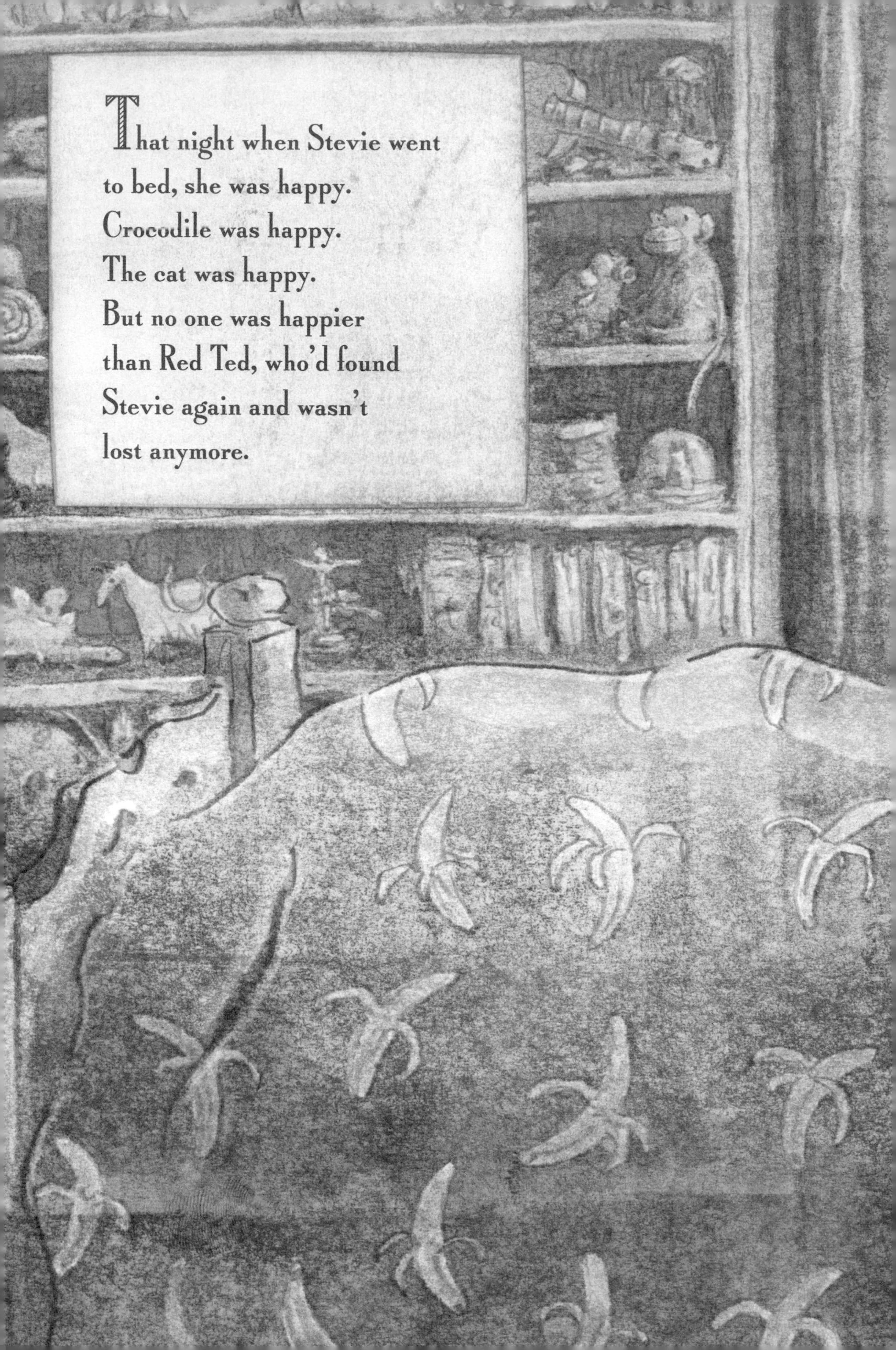

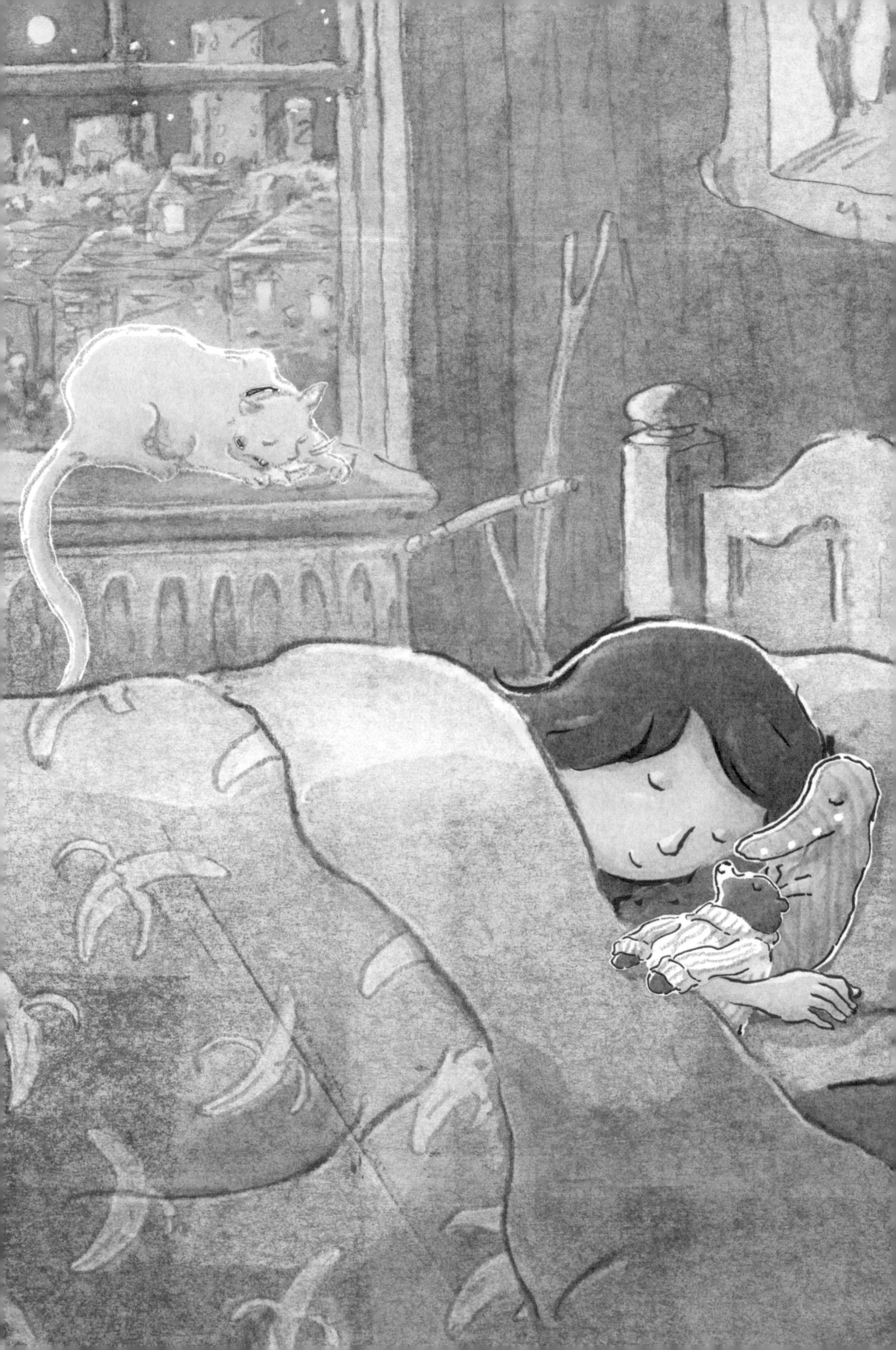

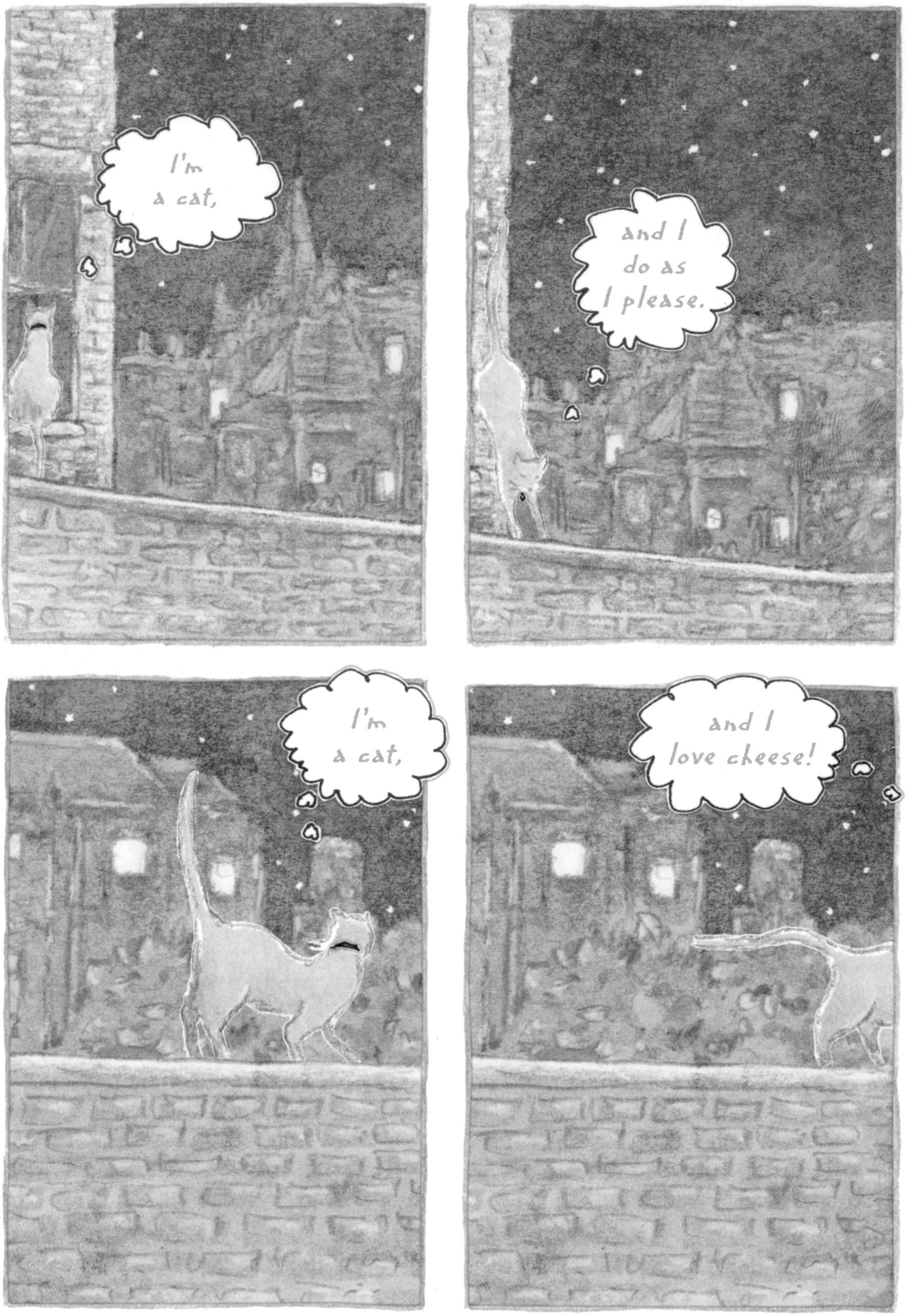
I'm a cat,
and I do as I please.
I'm a cat,
and I love cheese!